I Put Away Childish Things

CAROLE MARVIN

A DIVISION OF THOMAS NELSON
& ZONDERVAN

WestBow Press books may be ordered through
booksellers or by contacting:

WestBow Press
A Division of Thomas Nelson & Zondervan
1663 Liberty Drive
Bloomington, IN 47403
www.westbowpress.com
844-714-3454

Scripture taken from the King James Version of the Bible.

ISBN: 978-1-6642-3930-2 (sc)
ISBN: 978-1-6642-3932-6 (hc)
ISBN: 978-1-6642-3931-9 (e)

Library of Congress Control Number: 2021913315

Print information available on the last page.

WestBow Press rev. date: 07/30/2021

Dedicated to Sally and Tony who believed in me when I didn't believe in myself.

Thank you.

Contents

Prologue

The times and seasons of one's life are determined by many factors. Who we become depends on our determination to choose and our ability to develop a clear understanding of what we want and what we don't want. Our environment, our community, and the part of history we are born to contributes to our path in life. Whom we love and who loves us is another stitch in our fabric that God carefully adds to complete us. The McDonald family lived their life path in Evansville, Indiana. In the late 1930s, it was a growing city located on the bend of the Ohio River. The city had been founded in 1812 and had grown rapidly because of its natural resources and a large influx of immigrants who were ready and willing to work hard to provide for their families. Amid the Second Industrial Revolution and with the end of World War I, people had flocked to America to find a better life. Now the stock market crash of 1929 was a distant memory, and people were hopeful about building their great nation again. The families in Evansville, including the McDonalds, were hardworking, godly people who wanted to take their small piece of the American dream. The family has always been God's design for the advancement of His kingdom. The moments lived and stories remembered are part of the lifeblood of our existence. This story carries the message of a young woman who experienced love and loss, which sent her on a journey that led her to God and brought her to a place of redemption.

1
Chapter

I never considered myself a beautiful girl. My dad said I was his brown-eyed beauty. He would pat my head and say I had hair the color of wheat in sunshine. He always called me his number one girl. I was, in fact, his only girl. I guess I was just the same as any teenager growing up in the late 1930s. I had dreams and desires that were important to me. I had no idea what life had in store; I just wanted to have fun like most kids. I was getting ready to graduate from high school and was looking forward to the lazy days of summer. I wanted to live it up and enjoy my life.

Since I was thirteen, my parents had depended on me to help around the house and tend to my little brothers. I was sick of housework and tending to little kids. I didn't mind helping them as long as I could go out dancing on the weekends, but I wasn't ready to settle down and start keeping house, even though I had a boyfriend whom I loved and who loved me. We were both getting out of school, and our futures looked bright. It was a great time to be alive.

I never thought much about grown-up issues. I always figured my parents would take care of me because that's what they had always done. Jack, my boyfriend, was ready for married life, but not me. I was a young woman on the brink of great possibilities, and nothing could slow me down. Life was to be lived and lived to the fullest. I think most of my philosophical ideas came from magazines; nevertheless, I headed into the future with my eyes full of stars and dancing shoes on my feet.

My main interest was learning all the new dance moves. I loved the big bands and could master almost any new dance. We were at the peak of the swing era, and I could jitterbug better than any of my friends. Benny Goodman was my favorite. I could hear him on the radio, and sometimes I could pick up Glenn Miller and Tommy Dorsey. This music drove me like a moth to a flame.

We were not a rich family. My dad worked for the railroad and made a decent wage. I had everything a girl could want. I had a family who loved me and a great boyfriend. I was looking forward to graduating and getting a job. I wanted to be free to do anything I wanted when I wanted.

———— ❈ ————

"Dad, the water is only coming out in a trickle again. How am I going to wash these dirty plates with no water? Dad, hit those pipes again—the water is still not coming fast enough! When is old man Johnson going to fix our plumbing?"

I am so sick of this. I'll never get these dishes finished! I want to go downtown today and do some shopping. Woolworth's has some new lipstick colors, and Mary Ellen and I want to get first pick.

"Georgie, let Sammy go! You know he isn't as strong as you. Every time you hold his head down on the floor like that, you get his heart racing. You know he's got a condition. Let him go!"

"He's always taking my candy, and he *never* does anything to earn it. I pick up bottles all day, and all he ever does is play, and then I have to share with him! It's not fair, and I'm tired of giving to him, and all he does is shoot marbles!" Georgie shouted.

"Leave him alone. He has a condition. Dad, please hit those pipes again before you go to work!"

"All right, Gracie lass, but I don't have much time. I can't be late today because I get paid time and a half on Saturday. Make your mum a cup of tea; she is having a hard time getting up this morning. The baby is pressing on her back, so she needs to stay in bed. Gracie girl, you need to stay home today and tend to your mum and your brothers. Her time is getting close."

"Dad, you know this is the only day I can do what I want, with school and the household chores."

"Not today, Gracie. You're the only one I can count on; you're my number one girl. Boys, go outside and give this lass some peace. Georgie, you had better go down to Eighteenth Street today. I hear the neighbors had a party the night before last. There should be lots of beer bottles lying around. You know how Stu likes to raise his elbow with his friends. Gracie, I got to go. You know we need the extra money to pay for little Kenney's funeral. Even though he was just three years old, those funeral homes don't drop the price on those wee boxes. It still hurts my heart to think of that sweet lad dying so young before he had a chance to live. Pray for your mum. She still can't stop thinking of him, even with a new one on the way."

My mama, Emma McDonald, was having a real struggle coming to terms with little Kenny's death. He had been a precious little boy with white curls all over his head. I would listen to him say his prayers at night and sing his nursery rhymes. He always gave me a good-night kiss and said, "I love you, Gracie." He was so delighted with Toby, the cat. He would call Toby, and the cat would follow him wherever he went. It's almost as if the cat knew that Kenny was not long for this world.

His cold had started in January. It had seemed extra frigid last winter, and the house never seemed to get warm enough. By the middle of February, the croup had set in, and Kenny started developing a fever. Many of the neighborhood families were suffering from influenza and pneumonia, so doctors were busy trying to care for the most serious patients. By the time the doctor could see Kenny, his condition bordered on critical. He was admitted to the hospital when his chest became so congested that he couldn't breathe, and pus pockets had built up in his lungs. The medicine did not seem to arrest the infection, and he deteriorated quickly. He died the second week of March, and none of us understood why this had happened to this sweet little boy. I still thought about him all the time, but my mum couldn't get over it, and I doubted she ever would. We'd all tried to go on with our lives, but Mum was pregnant again, and I knew she feared bringing another baby into the world. She had to keep functioning every day in spite of the pain in her heart. She hurt in ways I couldn't understand. How did you ever get over burying your baby? I heard Mama crying softly many nights, questioning God and asking why He had taken her baby boy so young.

My mum was a strong woman of faith. Her relationship with God was personal and committed. She had given her life to Him as a young girl, and she had never taken it back. She had always taught me to trust God in all situations and know that He had a plan and purpose for us all. I loved my mum, but I had never had her faith. I was more like my dad; I could take it or leave it. Mama got through her days now with God's help, but I could tell by looking at her that she was just going through the motions because her heart had never stopped aching.

If I could describe my mum to you, I would have to say she was the closest thing to a saint I'd ever met. She always had a kind word and a gentle way about her that melted hearts. She was about to deliver her fifth baby, and she was only thirty-five years old. She never complained and always had a way of making you feel better no matter what you were going through.

"Mom, I brought you a cup of tea. Dad said you were having a bad day."

"Yeah, this little one is strong and feisty; it kicks all night most of the time. I heard the boys fussing this morning. What was it about?"

"Oh, you know, the usual. Georgie is mean to Sammy because he has to share his candy, and Sammy wants to play and never do anything to help."

"Those boys will grow up and be great friends one day—you mark my words," Mama said, nodding her head.

"I hope you're right; then all this fighting would be worth it!" I told her I was heading to the store and would have lunch with her when I returned.

Georgie, my younger brother, was lost in his own thoughts most of the time. He spent most days looking for bottles in yards and alleys to get the one-cent deposit. His main goal in life was to make money. The school year was almost over, and Georgie couldn't be happier. He thought school was a waste of time. Mrs. Price, his teacher, picked on him because he was always instigating something. He had earned a reputation for being the biggest problem in the school. Mr. Wilfong, the principal, had told him the last time he was in the office that that was his last warning. The next time he saw him, Georgie would be gone for the rest of the year. Georgie told me that he had news for Mr. Wilfong: he was out of there—now. He said he wasn't going back this year or ever!

He didn't want to sit and read "dumb books" all day when he could be out making money. He had a hissy fit one day and yelled, "I been picking up bottles and junk since I was eight years old. I don't need anyone telling me what to do with my money. I'm not sharing with Sammy either. He needs to make his own money. I don't care what they say in Sunday school. I'm pretty sure God wants people to work and earn their own money. I saw in the Good Book somewhere where it says if a man doesn't work, then he doesn't get to eat. That makes sense to me."

Georgie's best friend, Freddie Morgan, lived just a block down. Freddie had seven brothers and sisters. His dad worked for the same railroad as my dad, the South Shore Line Railroad. He worked with the freight on the loading dock. This was a family that had known its share of heartache. About two years ago, they'd had family members, including Freddie's grandparents, sailing to the United States on a passenger ship from Scotland. A storm rose at sea, and the ship capsized, and everyone was lost. Freddie still teared up when anyone spoke of it. Freddie was a really funny little kid. He always complained about his sister Sadie. He said she drank all the milk, and he was constantly running to the store. He thought she needed a cow of her own.

"We got eight kids in our family, and none of us drinks as much milk as she does. Mom says she's growing into a woman, and she needs lots of milk. I think she just thinks of herself and no one else."

He made us all laugh with his comments about his family. I guess there were lots of complaints to go around in a family that large. Freddie was a good friend to Georgie, and he entertained us most days. There were a lot of Scottish families in our neighborhood, and we understood each other.

Georgie would spend most of the morning checking the vacant lots and alleys, looking for anything he could take to Bill's Junk Yard and turn into cash. You could bet your bottom dollar Georgie and Freddie would show up for lunch when I got back with the soup; they always did. I felt sweat running down the back of my neck. I lifted my hair, and the old thoughts started whirling around in my head. *Here I go again, doing all the work. This family depends on me to do everything.*

Every time I thought about that new baby, I got anxious. I knew I was going to get stuck with all the work and chasing those two unruly brothers! I wanted a life of my own, and I felt like it was about time. I wanted to dance and have fun. It was the only thing that made me happy right now. Whenever big band music came on the radio, I got so excited. I just wanted to dance and enjoy my life. Was there anything wrong with that? I guessed I was a little stubborn, but a girl had to stand up for herself. I wanted to be strong and levelheaded like Dad said, but I wanted to have fun too. I was a good girl, I respected my parents, and I would never disobey them. I just wanted to stand my ground about things I cared about. I was grown up now, and it was time for me to start living like it. As far as my parents were concerned, I would always consider their wishes, but I was eighteen, an adult, and that meant freedom.

"Mum, I'm back, and I'm going to start the soup."

"I'll be down soon, dear," Mom said slowly. "The boys were here and already had something."

I slammed the refrigerator door as Mum wobbled into the kitchen.

"What is it, dear?"

"Mum, you are never going to believe this. That boy has less brains than God gave a duck! I think Georgie and his buddy Freddie ate the cat's food for lunch!" I stared at Mum in hopeless frustration.

Mama looked a little stunned for a moment. She began to smile as she lowered herself to a chair and then fell back into uncontrollable laughter. I couldn't hold it back either as Mum said, "That's why I never worry about Georgie. He knows how to take care of himself. The boy has never missed a meal in his whole life."

We laughed until Sammy came into the kitchen and said, "Is there anything else for lunch besides soup?"

We started laughing all over again. "Oh yea," I said, "we have other options, brother. What are you hankering for?"

2
Chapter

My dad had been at his job for twenty years, and he was good at it. He worked hard because he had a powerful desire to provide for our family, and he was an honorable man and well respected. On the job he gave all he had to the railroad and his fellow workers. It was not just a job to him. It was a commitment to contribute to something bigger than himself. My dad had lived through the Great Depression and World War I, and the impression these experiences had made on him had forever changed his life. He paid close attention to the newspapers and the radio, concerned always with the state of our country. His ancestors might have come from Scotland, but he was an American now and proud to be one. He had seen people suffer and go hungry, and he never wanted to see his family and friends fall into a state of despair and hopelessness again.

Dad was responsible for signaling trains coming into the station and keeping them on the right track. He was a strong man, not just physically, but in ways that mattered. He had said over and over that he wanted his kids to grow into strong, good people who were well respected in our community. He believed we needed to be thankful that we lived in America and had opportunities that people in other countries didn't have.

What really impressed me about my dad was how he treated

my mother. He told us over and over that he'd known from the first moment that he met my mama that she was the woman he wanted to spend the rest of his life with. He worked hard for her and his kids. Some men had big dreams and aspirations of doing great things, but my dad just wanted to love his wife and build a life for her and his family till the day he died. Allowing me to see how he loved my mother was the greatest gift he could ever give me and the best example he could ever set.

They taught us in school about the state and city we lived in and all of the benefits we had as a growing community. We learned about the people and the kind of work they did. This bored me to tears, but I guess it was necessary to understand why people must work to make a living. As for me, life was too short to think about working all the time. Life should be lived without worrying all the time, especially while we were young.

In our history class, we learned that most of the people who lived in the United States were from other countries, like Ireland and Scotland. Our family's ancestors came from Scotland, according to all our relatives' stories. Our family had been here for a few generations, so we were 100 percent American. We were a stubborn lot but would give our lives for family and maybe a few friends, if they proved themselves worthy.

Evansville, Indiana, where I lived, was a city composed of neighborhoods of various ethnic backgrounds. It was not uncommon to find Polish families living right next door to Italian and Irish immigrants. They said in school that we were a melting pot. I guess that meant we blended into one big pot and helped one another, or so it seemed. In school one of our textbooks called our country a miracle. It said the nation was growing and developing into a way of life where people accepted one another's differences and worked together with people different from themselves. According to our teacher, the large bend in the Ohio River had proved to be a big help to the industry of our town. People were working and hopeful about their futures. The country was at peace, and the hardships of the past were a distant memory. Our city had the ability to move products to market easily because of the river and our central location. We were going to grow to be a large city one day. Companies here made automobiles and refrigeration units that everyone craved, and the railroads could ship these items all over the country. Thousands of jobs for skilled and unskilled workers were created for many people who were not educated. To obtain a good-paying job without a high school diploma was a blessing and the financial salvation of many families. When you got right down to it, our actual survival depended on it.

Tom Wilson was my boyfriend's dad. Jack said his dad had enjoyed working with wood since he was a young boy. His grandfather had taught him to carve boats and then build birdhouses when he was but six years old. He loved to smell the wood and run his fingers along the grain. He had realized at a young age that no two pieces of wood were the same; they were distinct and almost a work of art in themselves. He made his living by developing pieces of furniture that caught the eye of his friends and neighbors. It was little wonder that Mr. Wilson had taken the thing he loved most and turned it into a prosperous business. He had always been told, "Choose a job you love, and it will never seem like work." He had taken this idea to heart. He'd started with just two saws in his basement. As the business began to grow, he found an abandoned garage and hired a couple of boys from the neighborhood to help sand and stain his finished pieces. Mr. Wilson had a good head for business, so each opportunity that opened up gave him a stepping-stone to expand and move toward his dream of owning large furniture stores in all the towns in the tristate area. His business continued to grow steadily to seventy employees. With Jack graduating high school, Mr. Wilson's dream of father and son working together was finally within reach. Jack was the only son. He had two sisters, but his dad looked to him to be his partner and someday carry on the family business.

Jack was looking forward to graduating from high school. He

liked working with his dad but did not really see it as his passion or life's work. Jack told me that his only passion right now was me. He said he thought about me day and night. He said he had given his heart to me in the third grade on the carousel in the schoolyard, and he had never taken it back. Jack was a strong, handsome young man with clear blue eyes and a rugged jaw. He had a way of charming anyone he met with just his smile. He was ready to take on the world with no hesitation. He wanted to step into his future, whatever it was, with me by his side.

I loved it when Jack laughed; it was contagious. Sometimes we'd laugh till tears flowed down our faces over absolutely nothing. Jack took life in stride, but this lighthearted attitude was not to his dad's liking. Jack thought his sense of humor was a trait that would carry him through, no matter what twists and turns life had for him. He was a positive and genuinely happy guy.

"Come on, boy, start sanding that table. We need to move that piece to the stain shop. It's going to be an outstanding coffee table if you ever come down from the clouds and get to work. See how the lines run so perfect in the grain? Ah, it will be one of our best yet. What's wrong with you, boy? You seem not yourself. Are you sick?"

"No, Pa, I'm just tired with working here after school every day and getting ready to graduate. I got a lot on my mind."

When Jack told me about this conversation, he said, "How can I explain to my dad that you consume my total thoughts? I can barely understand it myself. My feelings for you, Gracie, are growing so strong. You are all I can think about. You're the most important thing in my life." Jack said his dad wanted him to succeed in business and take over some day and follow in his footsteps. He had trained his boy to work hard and keep his mind straight. Girls should be the last thing on his mind. Girls and all that stuff could come later, much later. He wanted Jack to get established and make money, and then he would have something to offer a wife.

I thought these were all good ideas too. I wasn't ready for marriage, but Jack had other ideas. He told me his dad had told him to slow down and not waste his time with girls; they would just hold him back. Jack said little did his dad know that the time he spent with me didn't just slow him down; it stopped him in his tracks.

I knew Jack's family didn't want us to be together. They were a family who had money and traveled in different social circles than we did. Jack's mother came from a family that had connections with the railroad. She had been raised well, including finishing school. Her family had money and were well thought of in the community. She had met Jack's dad when he was first starting out, and I think her father helped him financially to get his business moving. Jack and I talked about his parents, and he said there would come a day when he would have to confront them about our relationship. For now, he didn't feel they needed to know all his personal business. I didn't want to start a big commotion in his family, so I didn't talk about it much. It seemed to bother Jack more than it did me anyway. I could wait because this time in our lives was all about having fun. I wasn't ready to fight for something I really didn't want right now.

I loved Jack, and I did plan on a future with him. I loved the way he called me his golden-haired beauty and always put me first. Sometimes when he looked at me, my knees would shake. I had always considered myself strong-willed and determined, but sometimes he had a way of melting my heart, without saying a word. I loved this boy and would love him forever. He told me one time that one of the things he loved about me was that when I had a mind to do something, nothing could stop me. He said that when I had on my saddle shoes and my favorite red paisley wraparound dress and had fire in my eyes, I could conquer the world. He smiled and said I had certainly conquered him.

3

Chapter

I hauled the basket of wet clothes to the screen door and kicked it open with my foot. Toby the striped tiger slipped in just before the door could hit him. "Well, Toby lad, it's going to be slim pickings for you today. Georgie and Freddie ate half of your food," I said, smiling to myself.

I hauled the large basket down into the yard to the clotheslines that stretched from the porch posts to two opposite posts across the yard. These posts were pounded in the ground. Dad had created this area in the back of our house so that there was ample room to dry the clothes. On wash days these clotheslines were loaded and a great necessity for our large family.

We lived in a row house, just like everyone else in our neighborhood. These were two-story houses built side by side with a small backyard and a stoop in the front just big enough to comfortably seat two people. Anyone else who cared to visit had to sit on the steps leading to the sidewalk. It was very common to hear friends and neighbors yell across or down the street with greetings or information they wanted to share. Every house had the same structural design. The main floor consisted of two large rooms. The main room was the first room past the front door and usually was called the front room. This was where the family would gather to play games and listen to the radio. Next was the kitchen, and off that was the community bathroom. There were stairs off the kitchen that led to the bedrooms upstairs. There were just two large bedrooms. Mom and Dad's room was the largest, with a double bed for them and a small bed where Kenny had slept. The latter soon would be replaced with a crib for the new baby. The other bedroom was shared by my brothers and me. My bed was on the far wall, and my possessions were off-limits to my brothers. The boys shared a double bed and fought most every night until they fell off to sleep. I could hear them kicking and poking each other. This irritated me just like their daytime combat. When you got right down to it, everything about my brothers irritated me. This sleeping arrangement was another reason I was ready for a life on my own.

I was finishing hanging the clothes when I heard Bo McAllister call my name from his back porch two houses down. "Hey, Gracie, are you going down to the creek tonight? There is supposed to be a bonfire, and Jody Smith is bringing a radio so we can listen to Glenn Miller and dance."

"Yea, I'm hoping to make it. My mum is not doing too well, and my dad is working late."

"Sweetheart, you got to come. You are one of the best dancers. I want you to teach me to do the shag."

"I'll try, Bo, but you know how it is with my family. I am chief cook and bottle washer."

"Well, everyone will be there, and half the fun is watching you come up with those new dance moves."

Bo McAllister and his family had always been our neighbors. He and I had been schoolmates since kindergarten. Bo had been the first boy to rub finger paint in my hair. He loved to have fun just like me. We liked to dance and together had learned all the new dance steps. You might say Bo was the mirror image of me. I'd been dating Jack for three years, so there hadn't been any room for Bo in my love life, but he had always stood by, waiting for an opportunity to present itself. I knew he liked me, but I'd never had those kinds of feelings for him.

"Try to come tonight, Gracie—it's going to be a blast!"

Bo's family were very quiet, unassuming people. His younger sister was behind me in school, so I never really knew her. I had never seen his parents outside in the neighborhood visiting with their neighbors. They were very private people. How they had raised a boy like Bo was a mystery. He was the most outgoing boy I knew. There was never an event at which he didn't show up and become the life of the party. I liked him, but I loved Jack.

I headed into the house to check on Mum. As I climbed the stairs, I heard soft moaning coming from Mum's bedroom. "Mama, are you okay?"

"Gracie, I think it's starting. I'm beginning to feel contractions, and my back is paining me terrible. Maybe you need to run down the street to Mable McTavish's house and see if she can come up and check me."

"Okay, Mama. Are you going to be all right while I'm gone?"

"Yes, dear. But please hurry."

I knew that after a woman had had two or three babies, the next ones could come quickly. I did not waste any time running to Mable McTavish's house. Mable was the midwife for the neighborhood. She had delivered more babies than the local hospital. She didn't charge money for this service, but folks donated all sorts of things to her and her family. Mable was a middle-aged stout woman who had immigrated from Scotland as a young woman. She had maintained many of the attributes of her countrymen. She was strong and stubborn but loyal to her family and friends. If you needed anything done and done right, you called Mable McTavish. Mable had delivered all four of us, so Mama had faith in her and her experience as a midwife. Mable was a strong Christian woman and had been known to pray the birth mothers all the way through the delivery. She was kind of a mixture of a preacher and a doctor. We all loved her and trusted her with our lives.

I pounded on Mable's door as hard as I could. "Mable, are you home? I need ye. Mama's in labor."

The door swung open. "Is she having pain, lass?"

"Yea, she said there's pressure in her back."

"Ah, a back labor—they're the worst. I'll get my bag and be right along. You go home and get the water boiling."

Mable arrived not far behind me. She had everything she needed and could be instantly prepared.

Out of breath, we rushed up the stairs to Mum's bedroom. "Are ye feeling the pain, lass?"

"Ah, yes, Mable, something is definitely going on. I got lots of pressure in my back, and I feel dampness on my sheets. I think the water has come."

"Ah, let's take a look, dearie."

I ran downstairs to gather up some of the towels and sheets that they were going to need. I got the kettle of water off the stove and looked out at the front of the house to see if I could spot my brothers.

I hoped this baby would come quick. Sammy had come out in just two hours.

"Gracie lass, things are slowing down. This may take a while. You might want to find Georgie and send him to the railroad yard and let your dad know what is happening here."

"Yea, I will do that. Be back soon." Georgie wouldn't be that hard to find. Most afternoons he was either sitting against the wall at Joe's Grocery or playing stickball in Freddie's backyard. Sometimes he was picking junk, but that should be over for today.

"Georgie, I been looking for you. Mum is getting ready to have the baby, and you need to run to the railroad yard and tell Dad. It's moving slow, and Mrs. McTavish is with her."

"Okay, sister, I'll tell him." Our family could fight each other, but when a family member was in need, we all would move heaven and earth to get the job done.

I immediately knew that there wouldn't be any dancing for me that evening. I thought about calling Jack and letting him know that I wouldn't be there tonight. Questions raced through my mind. *Am I ever going to be free of this family and all of the responsibilities pushed on me?*

"Dad, Mum is having the baby—can you come?"

"Is Mable with her, lad?"

"Yes, sir, and so is Gracie."

"Okay, son, I'll let my boss know, and I'll head home. You run along and find your little brother. I'll see you at the house."

The pains were beginning to come more often, but there was still something slowing down the process. "Emma, I don't think the wee babe is in the right position. I may need to turn him a bit."

"Whatever you need to do, Mable. I am getting tired, and these pains are getting stronger. Please pray, Gracie. I know God can turn this around."

Mable grabbed my hands, and together we laid them on Mama's stomach and asked God to put this baby in the right position.

My dad wasted no time getting home. He burst through the front door and headed to the stairs, taking them two at a time. "Emma, are you all right?"

Mama was screaming against a hard contraction and wasn't even aware Dad was in the room. Mable looked my dad square in the eye and said, "Willie, go downstairs and pray for this lass and the wee babe. She will be fine. Things are starting to progress quicker now."

The whole family gathered, waiting for word from Mable and me. We were all scared because when all was said and done, Mama was the heart of our family. The labor continued getting more and more intense. Mama was screaming as this baby worked its way into the world. Mable said that this was a hard delivery. Maybe it was because Mama was a little older. This was hard on her, and she was exhausted.

A soft whimper came, followed by a loud cry, and everyone knew the baby had arrived. Dad hurried back up the stairs with the boys close behind.

"Well, now you have a fine healthy daughter, Willie, and a strong one as well. She took her good old time getting here but has promised to let you know she's here to stay."

Relief and joy flooded that room. We all crowded around, as everyone wanted a look at the new addition. "She looks like a wet cat," Sammy said.

Tears flooded my eyes. "I think she's beautiful, just like Mama."

As Mama leaned back, holding her sweet baby girl close to her heart, she said, "Well, it looks as if the good Lord has performed another miracle for this family. God takes away, but He surely gives back. Thank you, God!"

Finally, Sunday evening arrived, and I was free to do what I wanted. Dad was home with Mum, taking care of things. Mum was resting in bed and feeding baby Jane. It was the perfect time to take a walk with Jack.

"Gracie, let's walk down by the creek. I have been thinking a lot lately, and there are some things I want to talk about. You know graduation is next week, and then our lives are going to change drastically."

"Yes, I am so excited because now that Mum is getting back on her feet, I can think about going to Woolworth's to see if they need any new workers."

"Gracie, are you serious about getting a job?"

"Oh yes, it's my dream to get out on my own and finally do what I want to do. I want to earn my own money and buy whatever I want."

"Gracie, you know I love you. I always have and always will."

"Of course, I know that, Jack, and I love you too."

"I just thought after graduation we would think about our life together, maybe make some plans."

"Jack, we have our whole lives to think about our future. Let's have fun while we're young and free. I want to live while I can and not be tied down with responsibilities."

Jack stopped and pulled me into his arms. "Gracie, I love you so much that I can't bear to be away from you." He raised my head and slowly pressed his lips to mine.

I kissed him back and put my arms around his neck. I so loved kissing him. His lips were soft and sweet. He kissed me deeper, and I could feel his heart pounding in his chest.

"Gracie, please say you'll marry me."

I was stunned for a moment and pulled away abruptly. "Marry you? Now? Jack, I'm not ready to get married now. I want to live and have some fun. Surely, you don't want to settle down now. We just finished school. Don't you want to live a little?"

"You make marriage sound like a death sentence."

"Well, in a way it is! It's cooking, cleaning, and taking care of kids. Jack, I do that now. Why would I want to sign on to that before I'm ready?"

"Well, I thought you loved me. I guess you and I are on different pages of this book."

"Jack, we're in the same book, just different timelines. Please be patient with me."

He pulled me into his arms again and held me close. "Gracie, you carry my heart and soul. How could I ever live without you? I'll wait as long as it takes, and one day, you'll be mine completely. I just hope you don't make me wait too long."

4
Chapter

Mama had been on bed rest for a week, and I kept expecting her to gain strength and start getting up and about. She said her legs hurt, and standing on her feet caused pressure that was sometimes unbearable. Baby Jane was doing well, nursing longer each day, and Mama kept her by her side, constantly watching for anything that could be a problem. Fear had left its imprint on Mama because of little Kenny, and I guessed only time would heal that.

Graduation came and went, and all the kids were out having parties, dancing, and having one last hurrah before looking for jobs and getting serious about life. Everyone was having fun but me. I had been cooking, washing clothes and diapers, and generally running the household. Bo came over one night and shared all the gossip about what our friends were doing. He missed me and couldn't wait till things were back to normal in our family. Jack had started to work with his dad. He liked the work but missed seeing me every day. At school we had always had lunch together and could sneak a couple of kisses in the alley behind the school building. My days now were full of chores and holding baby Jane, and his was full of making tables.

Late one night, I was jolted awake, feeling as if I was hovering between sleep and reality. I was in a dreamlike state when I heard my mum yell out from her bedroom. I was out of bed like a shot and tripped over Sammy's shoes on my way out of the room. "Mama, what's wrong?"

Dad was by her side, holding her hand. "I'm going to have to call the doctor in the morning," Dad said. "Your mom's legs are swelled and giving her pain. It seems to start in the calf of her leg and shoot up to the thigh. I can't figure it out. She has never had any problems like this before. Go get her an aspirin and some water. Maybe it will help her sleep."

Mom looked so tired, with black circles under her eyes. It hurt me to see her suffer like that.

"Gracie, honey, I am so sorry we woke you. You have been working so hard every day taking care of all of us. You need your sleep," she said. Mama moaned as she tried to turn over onto her side, and baby Jane began to stir. Dad gave her to Mama to nurse.

My mind began to race. When was this nightmare going to end?

Morning arrived bright and early, with baby Jane sounding off like an alarm clock. Her cries of hunger seemed to be getting louder as she got bigger. She was a strong little girl and becoming more beautiful every day. She seemed to have my nose, but everything else was too early to tell. Dad went out early that morning because he wanted to stop at Dr. Evans's office to see if the doctor could come by and see Mama today. I had to stay home again with Mama so that the doctor could check her, and I could care for the baby.

"You two eat your cereal and don't say a word. Mama isn't feeling well, and the doctor is coming by later to check her. You find something to do outside of this house, or I'll skin you both."

"Okay, sis, no problem! Sammy, do you want to come with me and look for junk down on the creek bank?"

"No, I got a marble competition down at Joe Black's house today. We're playing for pennies so I can earn my own money and buy my own candy."

Dr. Evans finally showed up halfway through the afternoon.

"I've had a busy morning, Mrs. McDonald. Sorry I'm so late getting here. Willie said you got pain in your legs. Let's take a look." He examined my mum's legs. "That sure is a strange-looking situation. Can't say I have ever seen anything quite like that. What does the pain feel like? Is it a sharp jabbing pain or an aching dull pain?"

"It aches sometimes, but other times it's a sharp shooting pain, like a knife is cutting through me."

"Well, I want you to have your husband wrap your legs in gauze and make it pretty tight to help the swelling subside. Take some aspirin for the pain and stay in bed. You got a fine healthy girl here to help out with things around the house. I'm sure you'll be fine in a few days."

After the doctor left, Mama called me upstairs to her bedside. "Gracie, I know this has been hard on you. I am so sorry that I haven't bounced back as quickly as I had hoped. I'm praying, and I believe soon I will be as good as new."

"I understand, Mum. I don't fault you."

"Gracie, are you still seeing Jack?"

"Oh yea, I love Jack, Mum, but he is so serious. He talks about marriage and spending our lives together. I'm not ready for that. I want to have fun. He doesn't quite get me. I want to earn some money, have some fun, and then settle down."

"Jack is a good boy, Gracie. He'll make a fine husband someday when you're ready. I just want you to be happy, my sweet girl."

"I love you, Mama. What would I ever do without you?" I did love my mama, but I was tired of carrying the load for this family. Why did all of this fall on me? What about my life and my wants?

Mama's legs were not getting any better. She could barely get down the stairs to the bathroom. Old Doc Evans came around the next week and talked to her about something called "milk leg," whatever that was. He said she should bounce back in a couple of weeks because she was strong.

Just a few nights later, I woke out of a sound sleep to screams and other noises coming from my parents' room. Mama was crying, and Dad was trying to calm her down. Baby Jane woke and was also crying to be nursed.

"Can I do anything, Dad?"

"Gracie, take the baby downstairs and see if you can put a little warm milk in a bottle and feed her. Maybe she'll go back to sleep."

Mama's legs looked bruised and swelled. She was in excruciating pain, and fear radiated from my dad's eyes. I knew something was wrong, and it was bad. I snatched up baby Jane and took her to the kitchen to feed her and calm her down. I could hear Mama crying upstairs and the floor creaking as Dad paced back and forth, trying to figure out what to do next. Jane fed and drifted back into sweet baby slumber. Things grew quiet upstairs, and I began to calm down. I took the baby back up to Mama.

"Gracie, I want you to keep the baby in your room tonight," Dad said. "Make a pallet on the floor for her. Mama needs to rest tonight."

"Okay, Dad." I took a quilt and made a soft bed on the floor. Jane slept through till six the next morning. I got her up and had headed downstairs to warm more milk when I heard my dad yelling at Mama.

"Emma, Emma, wake up! Oh no! Not Emma!" My dad screamed like I had never heard before.

Both Georgie and Sammy came running down the stairs, their hair standing straight up. "Gracie, what's going on?" screamed Georgie. Both boys had just woken from a sound sleep.

Sammy said with tears in his eyes, "What's wrong with Mama?"

"I don't know." I laid Jane on the couch and raced back up the stairs to my parents' room. I was not prepared for what I saw. Dad was lying over Mum, sobbing and mumbling something I could not understand.

"Dad, what's wrong? Please, Dad, what's wrong with Mama?"

I had never seen my dad cry before, and this was more than crying. He was desperately pleading with God not to take my mama, his Emma, the love of his life. My dad was frantic as he held my mama in his arms. "Gracie, Mama's gone. Mama is gone, Gracie!"

I fell to my knees in disbelief. "Mama can't die! She just has sore legs. She'll be okay in a few days—Doc said so." I felt my chin begin to quiver.

By this time, Georgie and Sammy were in the doorway, holding on to each other and sobbing quietly. My mama was the life blood of this family. Everything revolved around her. She was love personified. Never in her life had an unkind word come out of her mouth. She fixed every problem, wiped ever tear, and could always say the right words to heal your heart, and now my dad had said she was gone. How could this be? What would we do? The shock was more than any of us could bear.

The undertaker took Mama to the funeral home, and we were numb. I tended to the baby, and my dad stared into space. Mable came to the house and tried to talk to my dad. He couldn't think of what to do next. She tried to help him, and he managed to call my mother's sister Martha to tell her what had happened.

The funeral was five days later. Mama's sisters came in from Woodburn to help Dad and me with the funeral and the baby. My dad was in a state of shock. He had no idea what to do or how to do it. Aunt Martha basically took over and gave orders, which we all followed. The funeral was quick and included family and a few close friends. Neighbors sent food, and Mrs. McTavish organized the funeral meal. I walked around in a cloud, unable to believe that my mama was gone. How could this happen to the kindest, most unselfish person I had ever known? I heard someone say, "Only the good die young." I thought, *Doesn't God need good people to stay here and help out the rest of us? What good is it to leave all the bad people?* I didn't understand that then, and I don't think I ever will. Georgie and Sammy just sat in the living room, subdued and quiet. I didn't think they understood what it was going to be like in our home without our mama.

Aunt Martha and my dad were in the kitchen, having a real serious conversation, when I got up the morning after the funeral. Dad was shaking his head and wiping his eyes. Aunt Martha was trying to reason with him in the gentlest way possible.

"Emma wouldn't want that, Martha. She'd want her kids to stay together as a family."

Aunt Martha said, "How are you going to work and provide for these other kids if you have a baby to care for? You can't put that on Gracie, Willie."

"Gracie is a strong, responsible lass. You would be amazed what she can do."

"Yes, Willie, but is it fair to her? She's a young woman ready to start her life. Do you want her to stay home and tend to a baby all day every day? Think what would be best for the baby and Gracie."

The conversation subsided when they realized I was in the room. I started making some breakfast for everyone, and my dad abruptly left the room and ran up the stairs.

"Gracie, your dad is having a hard time right now. It's going to take some time for him to adjust to this tragedy."

"Aunt Martha, what were you and Dad talking about?"

"Well, honey, I was asking your dad to let me take baby Jane home to live with me and my family. It's going to be too hard for you all to tend to her. She is a newborn. It's not an easy job for a teenager and a dad who has to work every day. Then there are your brothers, who need to be kept out of mischief. It's not going to be easy on any of you."

I knew in my heart that Aunt Martha was right, but letting Jane leave would be like taking a piece of Mama away from us. We had lost her, and now we'd lose another piece of her. Our family had suffered too much loss in the last two years: first Kenny, then Mama, and now sweet baby Jane.

Aunt Martha stayed with us for two more weeks to get things in order. Dad went back to work finally, and a calm began to settle over our home. Georgie went back to picking junk, and Sammy involved himself in his endless marble tournaments with the neighbors. Aunt Martha and I tended to Jane, and she was right—it was a lot of work. There were diapers to wash and bottles to make and meals to cook. I hadn't seen Jack in three weeks. His family sent flowers and came to the funeral, but we had no private conversations. He was busy helping his dad, and I was busy being the mother of our family, or what was left of our family.

Finally, the day arrived for Aunt Martha to go home. She had two children of her own, and even though they were somewhat grown and didn't require all of her attention, her husband was tired of being both mother and father, and he wanted her to come home. It had been a month, and her family needed her.

I'll never forget that Sunday when Dad had us all sit in the front room for a talk. He started out by blowing his nose and wiping his eyes, as he did any time he had to talk about Mum. He started, "You all know that I love every one of you. No one is more important to me than you children. Aunt Martha and I have been trying to figure out how to keep this family going without your mum. I've racked my brain every day, looking for a way to keep us together. I'm afraid there is only one solution, and even though it grieves me greatly, this is what I must do for the good of us all. Aunt Martha will take baby Jane home with her to live with her family. We will visit as often as possible, but Jane needs to be with a woman who can tend to her. I can't put that burden on Gracie, no matter how responsible she is."

We all just sat there, stunned. We had lost our mum and now our sister. Even though we knew it was for the best, it still hurt to watch Aunt Martha pack up all of Jane's things. We all held her and kissed her goodbye. She still had that sweet smell on her, what people called the dew of heaven. To me it was the smell of Mama, who I knew was in heaven watching this family suffer through yet another loss.

5

Chapter

After Mama died, life became very much the same and yet very different. I was now the woman of the house, whether I wanted to be or not. The boys still fought, but I managed to ignore them most of the time. I caught Georgie smoking in the alley behind our house and told Dad. He didn't respond at all, and I began to see that he was oblivious to whatever the boys did. He brought the money to me for food and household needs and spoke very little to any of us. Dad seemed to be coming home later and later after work. We rarely ate meals together. I would cook for me and the boys, but Dad seemed to eat elsewhere or not at all. I smelled beer on him from time to time, and he went to bed early most nights.

We didn't attend church anymore. Church had been Mama's desire, and since God had taken her, I didn't have much to say to Him anyway. Our family was shattered in ways that could not be explained. Each member was trying to hold on to the little pieces of Mama that we had left. I found her Bible in Sammy's bed one morning. He must have slept with it. I didn't know how to help the boys deal with their grief. I couldn't deal with my own. There were moments when I would just sit down in the middle of the day and begin to weep. How could a loving God take a mother from her children? It made no sense to me.

Woolworth's did hire me to work at the soda counter. It

was not my favorite part of the store because once again, I was serving food to kids. I did earn money for myself, and even though it was a small amount, I could buy whatever I wanted for me, just me.

Jack still worked for his dad, who kept him busy. It was apparent that Jack's dad wanted him to spend as little time with me as possible. When we did see each other, he wanted to talk about our future. Our times together were strained and not much fun anymore. It didn't matter because Bo was always ready to take me dancing whenever we could sneak away. I liked Bo. He was a fun-loving guy with no pressure or commitments. He wasn't ready to settle down either. We agreed that life was short, so we needed to live it up while we had the opportunity. I used my social life to take my mind off of Mama. When I was dancing or laughing with my friends, I didn't think about the pain and heartache that had a stranglehold on our family.

"Gracie!" Bo yelled across the yard. "There's a huge party tonight down at the creek. From what I hear, it's going to be the biggest blast of the summer. Everyone is going to be there! Eddie Smith is bringing beer from his dad's stash."

"Really? Well, you know I'm ready for some fun. It seems like all I do is work. Can I walk down with you?"

"Sure, babe, I'm at your service. See you at seven."

Seven o'clock couldn't come fast enough. I had a new dress that was perfect for dancing. It had a full skirt so I could move easily. I had just bought a pair of low-heeled sandals that were perfect with the dress. I tingled with excitement. This was how a teenaged girl was supposed to live!

Bo and I moseyed arm in arm toward the creek. I could feel the excitement in the air. It promised to be a perfect evening. The air was warm, and the sun was low in the sky, and I was feeling exhilarated, anticipating all of the fun that I was about to enjoy.

We reached the center of the clearing where a fire was

beginning to build, and I was startled to see Jack there, his eyes fixed on me. He stared at me and Bo until we reached the fire. I hadn't thought he would be there. I'd had the impression his dad would have work for him, as he always did.

"Jack, I didn't expect to see you here tonight. I thought you'd be working."

"Yes, it's pretty clear you didn't expect to see me." His mood was somber and very serious. I rarely saw him like this, and it unnerved me to say the least. "Gracie, can we talk privately?"

"Sure, let's go over under that oak tree. Jack, I know how this looks, but you know Bo is just my friend and neighbor. There is nothing between us."

"Well, I had always thought that, but lately I see things a little different. I've seen the way he looks at you and how he is always drawing you out to some party or dance. People have told me that they see you more with him than with me. He wants to supply all the fun you crave and enjoy himself right along with you. You're different, Gracie, since your mom died. You've gone from being the most responsible person I knew to someone who doesn't consider anyone but yourself. You certainly don't consider me at all. I thought we were one, a couple destined to be together forever. I don't even know you anymore."

I could feel the anger raising up the back of my neck and exploding in my head. "Well, Jack, old boy, I lost my mother and really my dad too. No, I'm not the same person anymore. You and I are on different paths. I am taking care of myself and doing what's best for me. Haven't you heard the old saying 'look out for number one'? Well, I'm number one right now. Find a girl who wants to stay home to wash your socks and cook your meals. That girl's not me, and it never has been!"

All of the hurt and anger that had been building since Mama's death spewed out of me like a volcano. I needed Jack to understand, not chastise me. "No one ever sees how I feel or cares about what I want. Does anyone ever think about me?

No, you just think about yourself and your perfect family. You have everything, and everything I had has been taken away. Life slapped me right in the face, and all you can do is criticize me. Stay away from me, Jack. You don't understand, and I doubt you ever will."

Jack just stood there with tears in his eyes. I could see every hope and dream in his heart crash into the dirt on that creek bank. His precious, beautiful Gracie had turned into someone he didn't know and perhaps had never known. I didn't care how he felt. Life had given me a blow, and I was still reeling from the force of it, and I didn't need someone telling me I was selfish. I needed comfort, not correction.

Jack left the party, and I joined Bo, who handed me a cold beer.

I yelled as loud as I could, "Let's turn up the music and ring-a-ding-ding! This party is just getting started!" I didn't really like the taste of beer, but I drank it anyway to feel energized and confident that my life was all that mattered right now.

6
Chapter

I didn't see Jack for a couple of months. I was sure he was working with his dad and probably hated me as well. Our home was about the same, except Dad started bringing beer home with him and keeping it cold in the fridge. School was starting, and Sammy would get up and go most days, but Georgie refused to go back. Dad said that was okay as long as he found work to bring himself some income. He wasn't going to sit around all day and do nothing. I still worked three days a week at the soda bar and went out with Bo every chance I got. Bo was beginning to dote on me more and had even kissed me a couple of times. I wasn't interested in a relationship like that, but I needed someone to have fun with, so I just laughed it off. He was never too pushy, so I saw it as harmless fun. Somehow my family and I were surviving in spite of the heartache that still lived deep inside each one of us. Fun was my survival skill, and I used it as often as possible.

Our country was in turmoil, and everyone was feeling it. President Roosevelt had been speaking on the radio about the conditions in Europe. France fell to Nazi Germany in 1940, and the United States had begun building up arms to help our allies in Europe, China, and the Soviet Union. Money and supplies were being sent even though we had not signed on to fight another war. We had not forgotten the last war, and fear was rising daily because of the anticipation of being drawn into another one. Lots of the boys I had graduated with had already joined the army, knowing that it was just a matter of time before they would be called up. I knew my brothers were not quite old enough to be called on, so I didn't give the draft much thought.

I was busy mixing up a shake one Monday afternoon when I turned and saw Jack sitting at the end of the bar. My heart exploded in my chest. I hadn't seen him in months, and he looked older but, as always, outstandingly handsome.

"Hi, Jack. It's nice to see you. It's been a while."

"Yeah, I've been working every day. How have you been, Gracie?"

"Oh, you know, busy working here and taking care of things at home. Dad and the boys are good. Nothing new on that front. You look great, Jack. Working hard must agree with you."

"You're still as beautiful as ever. I don't think I've ever seen a girl as beautiful as you." Jack just looked at me with those piercing blue eyes. The depth of his feelings was quite clear. It was as if I could see in his eyes all the pain and all the hurt, and it hurt me to see him that way.

"Jack, I don't know what to say. You know I care about you."

"Yeah, well, I didn't come here today to drag up old feelings. I just wanted you to know that I joined the army, and I'll be leaving in two weeks. I go to Georgia for six weeks of basic training and then who knows."

I felt like a sledgehammer had hit me square in the chest. I was too shocked to speak, so I just looked at him, thinking, *No, you can't go fight in a war. I can't think about losing you too.*

I looked at his face but saw into his heart. Jack had been my best friend for years, and I knew him well. Exploding in my mind was the realization that I was the reason he had made this decision. I was the one who had driven him to choose war over being in the same town with me. The pain of us being apart was something he couldn't deal with.

"Jack, I'm sorry. I never meant to hurt you."

"Gracie, do you know what it's like to live in the same town with the girl you love and never see her? Sometimes you'll see her out at a club with another guy, but you can't bring yourself to say hi or engage in small talk because your heart feels like it's about to burst. The worst part is, as much as you want to, you can't touch her because she doesn't belong to you anymore. No, Gracie, that has been my life, and I have to get out of this town. I figure going to war can't be any worse."

"Jack, I do care about you. I just wasn't ready for—"

"Stop. I can't do this. I've got to go." Jack pushed back the stool. "You and Bo can have each other." He walked out quickly, and I saw him wipe his eyes.

I couldn't believe what was happening. I felt so guilty and responsible for all the hurt I had caused him. Mama used to tell me he was a good man, and now I had ruined his life. *Am I such a bad person? What is wrong with me? Is it so wrong to just want to have a little fun?*

7

Chapter

My life had settled into a mundane routine of cleaning, cooking, and working at my day job. I looked after the boys as best I could, but they had grown wild, doing whatever they wanted. Dad spoke very little to any of us and drank beer most every day. It was as if he was trying to dull his pain. I understood because I was in pain myself for many reasons. I had heard Jack left for basic training, and everyone was beginning to believe we were headed for war. Most nights, families sat around the radio, listening for the latest developments. President Roosevelt gave his fireside chats to keep us updated on the conditions at home and overseas. The folks in our neighborhood lived for the news because we all felt the clouds of war moving closer and closer every day.

I had increased my hours at the soda fountain, trying to earn some extra money for Christmas. The traffic in Woolworth's had picked up considerably with the Christmas shopping season approaching. I had been out dancing most every weekend with Bo, and we had upped our partying to include alcohol and a few cigarettes. I rather enjoyed the way a little beer or a highball made me feel. It seemed to numb the pain and guilt I felt most of the time. My mum was gone, my dad didn't seem to care what I did, and I never heard from Jack, so what did it matter if I drank a little and danced a lot? Bo was a great dance partner and a fun-loving guy. He liked to hold me close on the dance floor and would kiss me once in a while, but it was all in fun.

We had a swinging Christmas party planned at Jim Chapman's house. His folks were out of town, taking care of his grandmother. Bo and his friends were bringing beer and whiskey for highballs. We girls were bringing mixes and snacks. It was going to be the party of the year. I finished my chores around the house early so I could soak in the tub. My muscles ached from scooping ice cream all day. I had bought a new red sweater with buttons down the front. I pulled on my black skirt and platform shoes. I brushed out my hair so that it fell around my face, soft and flowing. I was getting comfortable with the party way of life. It required very little effort to show up, drink a little, and dance the night away. Sometimes I wouldn't even remember the next day whom I'd danced with, but I always ended up in Bo's arms at the end of the evening.

This particular night, we arrived right on time, and the music was already pounding. Some couples were dancing while Rosie Black and her boyfriend Joe were mixing drinks in the kitchen. I unloaded my contributions and headed to the front room to dance. Bo grabbed me, and we fell right into step with the music. It was a perfect night. All the conditions were right for a spectacular evening without a care in the world. I enjoyed my drinks and whirled around that room until I was dizzy. A few couples began to disappear, but I gave it no thought. I was having fun. This was what I'd always wanted. I guess I had a little too much to drink because before I realized it, Bo was leading me up the steps to a bedroom. He sat me down on the bed and began unbuttoning the front of my new red sweater.

I laughed at him and said, "Bo, what are you doing?"

"Just trying to give you some air. You got a little dizzy downstairs, so I thought maybe you needed to lie down."

"Yea, sure, I guess I drank a little too much. You're such a good friend, Bo."

Things began to get fuzzy, and I can't really remember all

that happened next, but I woke sometime later with Bo next to me in bed.

"Bo, what happened?" The realization of the situation began to work its way into my conscious mind, and I sat up, confused and dazed. "Bo, what did we do?"

"Now, Gracie, don't get upset. We had a good time, and you know I care about you. I've always loved you. You know that, right?"

The overwhelming truth of what had happened to me hit me like a hot iron. My fingers turned to ice, and I climbed out of bed and hunted for my new red sweater. I got dressed and got out of there quick. All the way home, I kept trying to remember what exactly had happened. I knew deep down that I had gone too far. I had never gotten involved in a physical relationship with Jack or any boy. I'd always thought I'd save myself for marriage like Mama had taught me. Well, I guessed I had messed that up now. I couldn't believe Bo had taken advantage of me like that. I'd thought he was my friend. Some friend!

Dad and the boys were sleeping when I got home. Thankfully, I didn't have to deal with them. I climbed the stairs and took off my clothes. After I was buried under my blankets, the tears began to flow. Mama would be so ashamed of me. Something had to change in my life. I'd made a mess of everything. I sobbed and sobbed until sleep overcame me.

The next morning, daylight came as it always did. It was a cloudy Sunday morning. Since none of us went to church anymore, everyone slept in as usual. I crawled out of bed feeling sick to my stomach and with a headache that promised to take me back to bed as quickly as possible. I had never in my life felt so sick and ashamed of who I was. I had always been a good girl. Maybe I was a little stubborn, but still good inside, like Mama had always said. She said God loved me, and I had goodness in me. I didn't feel good now. I felt a deep realization that I was lost and unloved and totally alone. "Mama, I need you! I have no one to talk to. When I lost you, I lost everything.

Help me, Mama!" I went downstairs and found the aspirin bottle and managed to down a couple and some water. I heard Dad moving around upstairs, so I hurried back up and climbed back into bed. I didn't want to look at or talk to anyone, not now or maybe not ever.

Late in the afternoon, I heard Dad and the boys talking. The radio was blaring, and my headache had subsided to just a dull pain. Even though my physical state was somewhat improved, my emotions were shattered in ways that I thought would never be repaired. *How could I be so stupid?* All this time, I had thought Bo was my friend, my dancing buddy. In my mind it had all been just clean fun. That was all I'd ever wanted to do—have fun. Bo must have had different ideas about me and our relationship. How could I ever face him or any of my friends again?

Dad called me from the bottom of the stairs, so I thought I'd better get up and tell him I was sick so he wouldn't ask a bunch of questions. "I'm coming, Dad."

As I reached the bottom of the stairs, my dad looked at me, his face as white as a sheet. "Gracie, we got terrible news over the radio. The Japanese just bombed Pearl Harbor this morning. They said on the radio that all of our ships and crews were likely lost. There were thousands of our boys killed or burned alive. Gracie, what are we going to do? This means we are back into another war."

I could barely hear my father talking. All I could think of was Jack, my Jack. My Jack, whom I'd told to stay out of my life and let me have fun. He was the only boy who had ever loved me enough to wait for me and protect me. He would have taken me home last night and made sure nothing happened to me. He never would have taken advantage of me.

It took very little time for our country to shift into the mechanics of war. War was declared immediately after Pearl Harbor, and young men from everywhere started signing up. Within weeks, all of my friends had signed the forms and were shipped off to various army bases for basic training. The general feeling throughout the country was anger and hatred for the "Japs."

I hadn't seen Bo for weeks, mainly because I stayed home most of the time except for work. I had talked to a few girlfriends on the phone to catch up on the news and to see if anyone had heard anything about Jack. No one had any news about him. I thought about calling his parents but didn't have the nerve. I assumed they blamed me for his decision to sign up. My life was deteriorating rapidly, and I was beginning to feel periods of panic set in, followed by a gnawing feeling of regret about Jack and how I had treated him.

8

Chapter

The winter was exceptionally cold, and the days were gray most of the time. I had a day off, and the sun was out, so I found a chair and parked myself on the back porch, where the sun could beat on my face. I had always been a sun worshipper; its warmth made me feel secure and relaxed. I leaned my head back and closed my eyes and tried to clear my mind of all the negative thoughts that plagued me constantly. As I drifted into a semi-conscious state, I felt a presence near me. I opened my eyes and saw Bo staring at me from the bottom of the steps.

"Bo, what are you doing here? I want you to stay away from me. Get out of my yard." I could feel the anger rising in my chest. My heart began to pound, and I fought back tears with fierce determination.

"Gracie, I'm sorry for what happened with us."

"You do not get to speak to me about that. You do not get to come in my yard and humiliate me again."

"Gracie, I didn't mean to let it go that far. You know I care about you. I've always loved you, since we were kids."

"What you did to me was not love. Someone who loved me would have taken me home and protected me. Someone with a shred of decency never would have taken advantage of me. Someone like Jack, who really loved me, would have shown respect. Get out of my yard, Bo, and don't ever come back."

"Okay, I'll leave, and you won't have to see me again because I leave for basic training next week. I just wanted to apologize and say goodbye."

I looked at him directly and saw remorse in his eyes, but it didn't change my feeling of contempt for him. I left him standing at the bottom of the steps and went into the house.

How could I have let myself get into such a mess? *What is wrong with me that I have stooped to such a low? I have shamed myself, my family, and most of all, my God. How will you ever forgive me, Lord? How will I ever overcome this selfish desire to do what I want? Look where it's gotten me!* I ran to my room, and thankfully, no one was at home. I fell on my bed and sobbed until I had to fight for breath. "God, I am so sorry that I ignored you. I'm sorry I never listened to Mama and went to church as she would have wanted. I have only thought of myself and having fun. Please forgive me, Lord, and help me. I don't know what to do. Please bring me someone who can help me. I have no one."

Days turned into weeks, and our lives began to change rapidly. Our whole country had shifted into war mode since Pearl Harbor. The men who could signed up to go fight, and the women were left to take over their jobs. I got a job on an assembly line at the International Steel factory. I worked the day shift, assembling joints for airplanes and tanks. Many of the large factories had stopped making things like cars and begun making airplane parts. We were at war, and our navy was badly crippled, having lost eight battleships and one hundred planes. We all had to do our part in keeping our country on its feet. Our whole culture had shifted from peace and prosperity to fear and anger. If there was anything that could be viewed as positive, it was the fierce solidarity that had united our country and propelled us into World War II.

There were times when Dad, the boys, and I would sit in the front room after dinner and listen to the radio. It used to be talent shows or farm reports, but now we all tuned in to the news about the war effort and what our troops were doing. Whenever President Roosevelt spoke, everyone hung on every word. My brothers would still go to the movies occasionally. Previously, you could pay five cents and watch cowboy movies all day. Now the movies were newsreels, and they were all about our war effort and pictures of bombings and troop movements. The boys started going less and less. This was not a fun time for kids or families whose men had left to fight for their country. My dad did not have to go because he was our only parent left since my mother's death. Dad stayed home and continued to work at the railroad.

Unfortunately, Dad continued to make beer his constant companion. At night I would hear him stagger to the bathroom and fall up the steps on his way to bed. I couldn't help him. I was drowning myself with guilt and shame, which culminated in total exhaustion. Georgie was gone most of the time. I never really checked on his activities. Mama had always said he could take care of himself, and I left it at that. My brothers needed guidance and a role model from their father, but that was never going to happen. Losing my mama had broken my father, and only God himself could fix him, and Dad had no interest in that.

I still went out on Saturday nights to the USO dances. It helped to talk to some of the soldiers about what was going on overseas. The music helped take my mind off of the pain and heartache I felt about Jack. I guess I felt if I was cheering these guys up a little, it was helping him in some unexplainable way. I danced, and I laughed, but I never again had a drink of alcohol. After my experience and after watching my dad every night, I had learned that was an avenue I needed to avoid. I volunteered at the Red Cross from time to time. I tried to keep busy because the more I did, the less my mind focused on Jack. I still didn't hear any word concerning him, but he consumed my thoughts every minute of every day.

9

Chapter

I had been so busy with my job and all the volunteer work that I hadn't paid much attention to my own health. I was tired a lot, and I was sick to my stomach. I threw up most days. I just kept pushing myself to keep all the nagging thoughts out of my head. I was coming out of the bathroom, where I had just brought up my breakfast, when Sammy walked into the kitchen.

"Yuck, you look terrible. Are you sick?"

"None of your business. Just make your lunch and go to school."

Sammy was almost fourteen by now and pretty independent. Neither of my brothers was old enough to sign up to fight, so I was thankful that I didn't have to worry about them. Sammy was spending a good bit of time at the local pool room downtown. The neighbors said he had a pretty good touch with the pool stick, and some even said he was a shark. I had little time to keep track of my brothers. I loved them, but I was not their mother, and Dad gave no thought to any of their activities. They were pretty much raising themselves.

Aunt Martha was coming to spend the weekend and bringing baby Jane. She was growing quickly. We had seen her only a few times since she'd gone to live with Mama's sister. Since Aunt Martha was coming to visit, Dad had tried to pull himself together and had gotten rid of all the beer bottles on the back porch. I guess Georgie took care of them for him for a price. Aunt Martha was a woman of faith like Mama. She didn't approve of using alcohol, and she did not hesitate to let her feelings be known.

I greeted Aunt Martha at the door, anxious to see Jane. "Aunt Martha, so good to see you. Baby Jane, look at you! Give her to me. I could just squeeze you to pieces."

Dad looked past me and gave Martha a hug. "It's good to see you, Martha. You look well."

Dad turned to me and reached out for Jane. I could see the tears beginning to form in his eyes. He and I knew that the more she grew, the more she looked like Mama. He held her close as he expressed more emotions than he had in months. I wondered if Dad would ever get over losing my mama. He gently kissed the baby's soft cheek. "She's growing fast, Martha."

"Yes, she eats well and sleeps through the night already. She is a very good baby, Willie."

Dad held her close, and I could feel what he was feeling. Being close to her was like being close to Mama. I could always feel what my dad was feeling. I was very in tune with him. I understood him, and our emotions seemed to mesh together into one.

The boys and I did have fun playing with our little sister. Her presence seemed to bring some joy back into our home. For a time, I forgot about the war going on outside and the bigger war going on inside of me.

As the evening progressed, I began to wonder if I might get a chance to talk about my inner turmoil with Aunt Martha. She had the same faith as Mama and understood God in much the same way. I had so many questions and so few answers. I had begun to see things differently, and I needed someone to help me understand. I tossed and turned all night, thinking about what I could say to her.

I finally got up before daylight to put on a pot of coffee. As soon as I began to smell the coffee brewing, the nausea began to rise, and I had to head to the bathroom again. As I came back into the kitchen, Aunt Martha was standing at the sink, rinsing out a cup, and our eyes locked.

"Are you sick, dear?"

"No, well, yeah ... I have been having some trouble with my stomach lately." I knew deep down that pregnancy was a possibility, but I had refused to think about it.

"Sit down, sweetheart. Let me fix you some coffee."

I knew in my heart that it was time to confide in someone. I knew Aunt Martha was a kind woman and would not think badly of me, no matter what I told her.

"I've had a rough couple of months," I said. "With the war and Mama being gone, it's been hard on all of us. Dad's not himself, and the boys are gone on their own."

"Gracie, how long have you been throwing up in the morning?" She poured cream into her coffee and looked straight into my eyes and straight into my soul.

I knew at that point that I had to reveal all the pain and anger that I had stored up for months.

"Honey, I'm not trying to pry into your personal life, but it seems to me that you are showing early signs of pregnancy. Is that possible?"

I could feel all the walled-up emotions beginning to break through. Those deep dark secrets that I had been hiding were shattering like a plate thrown against a wall. I couldn't stop the tears as they came out in spasms. "I ... I went to a party, and I ... I was drinking, and a boy took advantage of me. I didn't even know what was happening. I didn't mean to do it. I was confused and scared and don't even remember much of it." I sobbed like I had never done before. I could scarcely get my breath.

Aunt Martha let me pour it all out before she said a word. Finally, I calmed down, and she spoke softly. "Gracie, there is a very good possibility you are going to have a baby. Do you realize that you are going to have to deal with this?"

I tried to hold back the sobs, but they started again uncontrollably. "I don't see how that is possible. I barely remember what happened."

I could see the compassion and the sorrow in my aunt's eyes. My sobbing began to subside, and she took my hand.

"Honey, it only takes one time to get pregnant. Whether you remember it or not, it still happened. Now the question is, what are you going to do next? You are not a child anymore. You have to take responsibility for yourself and soon a baby. Do you have any idea what you are going to do?"

"No, there is no one to help me. I haven't told anyone about what happened. I am so ashamed, I can barely speak or think of it. There is no one I can turn to."

"Well, I certainly understand, but there is someone you can go to. Have you had a talk with God lately? Because He has all the answers."

"I don't know what to say to Him. I haven't spoken to Him since Mama died. He didn't see fit to save her life when I asked Him to, so why would He care about me now?"

"Honey, get yourself right with God, and He will tell you what to do."

"He's up there in heaven, I guess, so how can He talk to me?"

"God talks through people, so find a person who understands how He speaks, and let them help you to hear."

"I suppose I could go talk to Pastor Kirk at the chapel on Nineteenth Street. He came and talked to Mama when little Kenny died. I guess it wouldn't hurt."

"That would be a good idea, but the first thing you need to do is tell your father. He is the one who is going to carry the pressure of this and the financial burden."

I knew she was right, but fear began to take control of my whole body. I had never been afraid of my dad, but I knew he was not dealing well with Mum's death. I didn't know what another trauma might do to him. I had always been my dad's number one girl, so the disappointment that might come with this news terrified me more than anything. I loved my dad, and I felt his hurt because it was very much the same as mine. I didn't want to hurt him again.

I met Pastor Kirk after dinner the next week. He was a kind elderly gentleman. He invited me into his little office and offered me a cup of tea. I was so full of anxiety that I could not have swallowed anything. I could barely swallow my own saliva.

"My goodness, Gracie, it is so good to see you. How are your dad and your brothers?"

"Everyone is fine, Pastor. We are all just busy with everything going on in the country right now."

"Are you managing all right without your dear, sweet mama?"

"Yes, we miss her, but we're managing."

"So what brings you by today?"

"Well, to be perfectly honest, I don't where to begin. I guess I'll start at the beginning." For the next two hours, I poured out my heart about what had happened to me and all my anger toward God for letting my mama die and leaving our family on our own. I didn't leave anything out or hold anything back. I didn't know if he was ready for my tornado of emotions, but once I got started, I couldn't stop.

Pastor Kirk listened closely and showed very little emotion except for a sweet smile on his face. When I had calmed down and basically run out of steam, he spoke very gently to me. "Gracie, God has never turned His back on you because He loves so much. He has been watching you every day and waiting for you to come to Him. You see, lass, He has all the answers to life's problems, if we ask. You didn't ask Him for help when your mum died. You just got angry at Him and walked away and did what you wanted. He was waiting to comfort you and help with everything in your life, but you shut Him out. None of us can live our lives without the help of the Almighty. He wants to guide us and tell us which direction to go. He is kind of like a gyroscope that keeps us balanced and on the right path. That's why we come to church to learn how to hear His directions. There are pitfalls that we can fall into without guidance, as you well know."

As I blew my nose, I could see the tenderness in his eyes. I knew he loved me and was not at all shocked by what I had told him. "So, Pastor, what do I do now?"

"Well, my darling, are you still mad at God?"

"No, I guess not."

"Why don't you tell Him how you feel?"

I think this was the first time in my life when I had talked to God like He was there. I had said rote prayers on many occasions, but actually having a real conversation with God had never been part of my church life. I closed my eyes and started. "God, I hope you remember me. I haven't been to church for a while. I am sorry for not talking to you before. I really miss my mum; she was everything to me. I believe I have been mad at you for a long time, and I have made a mess of my life. I can't handle things on my own anymore, so I need help. I'm sorry for being mad at you. Can you forgive me and help me?"

The tears began again, but this time they weren't tears of shame. They were tears of release from all the weight of the pain that I had stored up for months. I felt the presence of God in that little office like I never had before. It was as if God had His arms wrapped around me and was taking all of the heartache and anger. I felt He was letting me know that everything would be all right. He would see me through no matter what happened. I guess I'd had an image of God that was distorted in many ways. I'd always felt He was trying to keep me from having fun and making me assume responsibilities. I had never looked at Him as a guide to keep me out of trouble.

Pastor Kirk looked me in the eye and said, "Gracie, God has a wonderful future for you. This is not the end but the beginning of a great life full of hope and purpose."

When I got home, Dad was sitting quietly in the front room,

and the boys were off doing something as usual. I took a chair opposite him and asked if he had a little time to talk.

"Of course, lass. I always have time for you."

"I have a bit of a problem, and it's time I told you about it." I could feel my stomach muscles beginning to tense up, but I knew it was now or never. "Dad, I really am sorry about this, but you have to know sooner or later. I went to see Doc Evans yesterday, and it seems I'm going to have a baby."

My father looked as if someone had hit him in the face. I had to drop my head because I couldn't look at him. I had always been close to my dad, and at times I could physically feel his pain. I could feel it now, and this revelation hurt him and me just the same. "Gracie, how did this happen? I haven't even seen you go anywhere for weeks."

I raised my head and looked into his eyes. The pain was evident, but so was love and concern for me, his little girl.

"Well, it happened right after Christmas at a party. I had too much to drink and made a big mistake. It was just one time, Dad, and I am so ashamed."

He quickly rose to his feet and drew me into his arms. This time we both wept for all of the loss and grief that had saturated our home and our hearts. The atmosphere in our house was thick with sorrow all the time, and we lived in it and breathed it every day.

"I'm sorry, Dad."

"I'm sorry too, honey. This is just as much my fault as it is yours." We wept in each other's arms until there were no more tears.

"Gracie lass, don't worry. We'll work this out. I love you, and nothing will ever change that."

I don't think I had ever loved my dad more than I did at that moment. I had always looked up to him, even though he had lost his way since Mama died. As he held me in his arms, my respect for him reached a whole new level, and I knew my earthly father and my heavenly one together would see me through this.

10
Chapter

The weeks passed, and I eventually stopped throwing up. I was thankful that part was over, but then I began to pack on weight, which really annoyed me. I was still able to work at the mill. There were many women working while pregnant; however, most of them had husbands who were off fighting in the war. The war raged on, and the women stuck to the news like glue. You could sense the fear every time a new front opened up. I knew the wives and mothers went home every night terrified that they were going to see a soldier at their door or a letter in the mail from the War Department. I still went to the USO occasionally. My friends kept telling me I was gaining weight. I had never told anyone that I was pregnant. I knew that eventually I would have to stay home and hide from the world. Being pregnant and unmarried was not acceptable.

One night, I was having a Coke with some guys and girls from our old high school class. Bill Tolliver said he had seen Jack Wilson the other day. Jack had been sent home because he was wounded. He had been hit with fire while running from the Germans in France. Bill had seen him with his dad downtown, walking on crutches. Bill hadn't talked to him long because he seemed to be in a hurry. My heart stood still. I could hardly believe Jack was home. I wanted to see him with every fiber of my being. I wanted to throw my arms around him and beg for his forgiveness. I wanted to tell him how much I loved him and was ready for the life he had offered me before he left. How could I do that while I was carrying another man's baby?

"Is he home to stay?" I asked. "I hear once a soldier is wounded, then it's over for them."

Bill shook his head. "Your guess is as good as mine. Things change from day to day."

The fear and anxiety that I had let go began to creep back into my heart. Jack would never want anything to do with me once he found out what I had done. I went home that night with a heavy heart. The old anger and grief began to build up again in my spirit. The only difference this time was that I knew I could call on God, and He would answer me.

I had a serious talk with God. "How can I ever hope to make things right with Jack? I have betrayed him in the worst possible way." The panic I often felt when I thought about Jack began to rise in my chest, but there was also a sense of peace that I couldn't explain. I had been attending the chapel most every Sunday, and I was beginning to learn about God and how He cared for the sheep of His pasture. I knew I was one of those sheep, and He would care for me too. Instead of crying myself to sleep, I prayed that God would work out His plan for my life with Jack or without him.

Every day was becoming the same as the one before. Going through a pregnancy without a husband to share it with was very lonely. I ached for someone to talk to. Dad and my brothers were caught up in their own worlds, and they didn't know what to say to me about mine. I was visiting the doctor once a month, and he said I was doing well. The baby was growing normally, and I should expect him or her by the middle of September. Jack never came to see me, and I was thankful for that.

Sammy began to concern me. He was spending all his time at the pool room downtown. According to Mable McTavish, the midwife down the street, he was playing pool for money. He had been competing in marbles and other games since

51

he was little, so this was no surprise. Now he was playing for money and gambling with grown men. Sammy and Georgie were rarely home for supper anymore, so I asked Dad if he knew that Sammy was spending all his time at the pool room and gambling.

"Dad, I'm beginning to worry about Sammy. He doesn't come home till late every night. I'm not sure he's going to school. I don't know who he is loafing with. The neighbors are saying he's a pool shark, and he's making a lot of money. He is really young to be hanging out with grown men."

"No, I didn't know he was gambling. I'll go down there and check on him. That boy needs a job. He has never cared to work and carry his own weight. I can understand why Georgie used to get so angry with him. Don't worry, lass. I'll take care of it. You just take care of you and the baby."

Sammy was a very likable young man. He was carefree and always had a joke to spring at a moment's notice. He had friends who followed him wherever he went. He was fun to be around, and his skill with the pool stick was the best in town, or so I'd been told. One of the neighbor boys told me that grown men would come from other communities just for the challenge of playing Sammy. Everything I learned about my little brother, I learned from the gossip in the neighborhood. Even though I lived in the same house, I didn't know what he had become in a short period of time. Sammy was young and very enlightened to the ways of the world. He could shoot pool and drink beer with the best of them. He could also dazzle the ladies with his charms. He had completed the ninth grade and figured he had learned all he needed to know from school. He had big plans for his life, and a high school diploma was not one of them. He, like Georgie, had quit school; he just hadn't told anyone.

Dad did follow through and check on Sammy. The next day, Dad didn't come straight home after work. Instead, as he would tell me afterward, he cut through the alley and headed downtown to the pool room. He didn't see Sammy when he first walked in, but he heard a commotion over near the pool tables. As he stepped through the crowd, he saw Sammy in a heated game with a man at least twenty years old. As Dad watched, his son cleared the table in a short period of time. The man handed over a roll of money, and Sammy turned to pick up his beer. When he turned back around, he came face-to-face with Dad.

"What are doing, son? Do you think you're old enough to be out drinking beer on a school night?"

"Dad, I didn't see you there."

"Yes, I am quite sure you didn't see me or expect me to be here. Put your stick away, boy, because you're going home."

I'll never forget the look on Sammy's face when he walked in the door that night. He was pale, and his eyes were wide and dark. His face looked like a blanket with two holes burned in it. He had been out all hours of the night for weeks. He hadn't been sleeping because he would get up early and pretend to go to school and then hide out all day and play pool all night.

My father was never one to get loud and hysterical, but when he was mad, he would get very serious and firm in his speech. "Boy, I had better never hear of you loafing at that pool hall again. If I hear you been playing pool for money and drinking beer, you'll answer to me. You think you're a big shot because you can win a pool game? Believe me, you'll only be a big shot when you can work and earn an honest living. You'll finish out this school year, and you will go back in the fall. Do I make myself clear?"

"Yeah, Dad, I hear you."

"Now go to bed, and we will not have this conversation again."

I felt a certain satisfaction in knowing I was not the only kid in this family that had messed up. I loved my brother, but sometimes boys had to be taken down a peg or two.

Life settled into an ordinary routine. Sammy finished school for the summer, and Dad made him get a paper route to earn money. Georgie had a day job at the junkyard, so he was bringing home a paycheck weekly. I was getting big, so I quit the factory and the soda fountain. I stayed home most of the time. I hadn't talked to any of my friends, so there was no word about Jack. I didn't know if he was still in town or had gone back overseas.

I didn't want him to see me like this, so it was just as well that he didn't come around. Things were better in our house. Dad was drinking less and taking more interest in our family. I think Sammy's escapade had shaken my dad up because now he kept his eye on both boys.

The baby was kicking and moving around more every day. I spent many afternoons with Mable McTavish, asking questions and gleaning knowledge from her about bringing a baby into the world. I was somewhat aware of what to do after a baby got here but completely ignorant about my role in the delivery process. She had been a midwife for many years, so her vast knowledge was greatly appreciated. This was a time to take good care of yourself, she said.

Mable was my best friend. She shared her experiences and her family with me. I was no longer the selfish young girl who just wanted to have fun. I discovered that the world did not revolve around me and everything I wanted for myself. I guess somewhere in all the chaos of life and loss, I had grown into a woman. I had moved past the selfish way I used to think. I was about to become a mother, and I was beginning to care about my baby more than anyone.

Mable's children were grown except for Alice, her youngest daughter. Alice was a senior in high school, and because there was little difference in our ages, we got along well. She liked music like me, and she kept me up on all the styles in clothes. Even though I was as big as a house, I could still dance pretty well. We would turn on the big bands and dance in her living room many afternoons. She made me laugh by telling me about all the stupid things that the boys in her class did. Mable's house was like a refuge for me. I felt safe and accepted there. It was like a little family outside my real family. I felt mothered and loved. Those afternoons gave me a sense of security and peace. Mable was also a strong woman of faith who had a wealth of knowledge about the ways of God. I loved those two women. They were my friends at a time when I needed them desperately.

August turned out to be hot and humid. They said on the radio that the temperatures were expected to hit ninety degrees and that the heat wave would last for a couple of weeks. I was more miserable than I had ever been in my life. No matter what I did, I couldn't cool off. Some afternoons I would climb into a tub of cold water just for a small bit of relief. When I went to the doctor for my regular checkup, he said the baby could come at any time. I needed to prepare myself and prepare Mable. Dad had given me a little money so I could buy a few diapers and blankets. He switched rooms with me so I could use baby Jane's crib. He said it would be more private for nursing the baby at night. My dad was so very kind to me during this time. I couldn't have asked for more support. Even my brothers were extra nice. It could have been that they were afraid that I would release my wrath on them if they messed up—I could be a little moody during this time. I worried constantly, not sure I could deliver a baby, let alone raise one.

I woke up at 3:00 a.m. in early September to a squeezing pain in my stomach. I lay there for a while because Mable had told me that sometimes there was this thing called false labor. The feeling came and went for the next three hours. I also had lots of pressure in my back, like Mama had had with Jane. Finally, I got up and went to the bathroom. Water began to gush out of me, and I knew it was happening. I got Dad up, and he went down the street to get Mable.

Once Mable walked in the door, I felt better. This woman had become my security in a life of insecurity. She was my rock. Of course, she had brought her bag with everything necessary to bring this baby into the world. After I was safely back to bed and checked, we all began to wait. Dad stayed home from work, and the boys, looking scared, stuck around too. As a family we had experienced so much loss, so no one was leaving until they knew everything was all right. The waiting game commenced, and this baby took its good old time. It was not until seven that evening that my baby girl fought her way into the world, kicking and screaming. She was a full eight pounds with a mass of dark hair that looked as if it needed a trim. Her little fists were clenched like a boxer ready for a fight. I was completely exhausted; I had been up sixteen hours. Mable cleaned her up and tucked us both in for some much-needed rest.

Dad and Mable took care of us for the next couple of days. I began to slowly recover and nurse my little peanut. She was truly beautiful. I held her close and felt the warmth of her sweet little body next to me. I loved her already. Until now, I hadn't understood what my mama felt about little Kenny or Baby Jane. She had loved us all, but there was something about a newborn or a young child that brought out that need to protect, that powerful force that would make you die for that baby. I felt that for my little girl, and I knew Mama had felt that for all of us. Mama used to say, "God equipped mothers with instincts to protect their young, and no one understands it until they have one of their own." She was right, and I knew nothing would hurt my little girl if I had breath in my body.

As the days passed, I recovered quickly and got into a routine. Peanut grew slowly and was a joy every day. Dad came home right after work every night now, just to see her. The boys were much quieter in the house. They would hold her while I made dinner and talk to her when no one was looking. It was hard to explain, but it seemed as if she was bringing peace and healing to our home.

One night after dinner, Dad said, "Gracie, when are you going to give that girl a proper name? You still haven't filled out the form for her birth certificate."

"I know. I have to make a decision about this soon. They only give you a couple of weeks to file the paperwork." I knew her last name would be McDonald like mine, and I had known in my heart the name I wanted from the beginning. I hesitated because I didn't want people to get the wrong idea about her father. But time was running out, and I had to name my little peanut. I filled out the form and took it to the city building and officially declared Emma Jacqueline McDonald into public record. I would call her Jackie because that name was close to my heart, like she was.

11
Chapter

The war continued to rage in Europe. Germany invaded one country after another. We were all glued to our radios as we prayed for this madness to end. Our boys were being sent all over the world to fight, and many were coming home in boxes when they were just twenty years old.

I prayed constantly for Jack. I hadn't heard any word about him. I had no idea where he was. I guessed I'd lost the right to have news about him a long time ago. I stayed home most of the time, tending to the house and Jackie. I gave her the name Emma because of Mom but I never called her that because Dad still had a hard time hearing the name of his dear Emma spoken out loud. I still was sensitive to his feelings. He was beginning to heal, and I didn't want to hinder him in any way.

The season was beginning to change, so I took advantage of the good weather most days to take my little peanut for walks in her buggy. She was a good baby, and we both enjoyed the warm sunshine. I was also trying hard to get my shape back. I usually walked three blocks down to Mable's house, circled around, crossed the street, and came back up the other side. Today I cut through Alley H to the next street down. I wanted to extend my time outside because it was such a beautiful day. I saw another mom coming toward me, pushing her baby. She must have felt the same need to slim down as I did. As she approached, I began to recognize her. I hadn't seen her in a long time, but I knew she was Bo McAllister's sister. She had married Robbie McGill before he left for the war. My heart ached for her because she was going through the same thing as me—well, not quite the same.

"Hello there. Aren't you Annie McAllister?"

"Well, it's Annie McGill now. Robbie and I got married before he went to the front."

"How is he doing?"

"He's doing okay. I get letters pretty often. I miss him terrible, and he has yet to see little Robert. Is your wee one a boy or a girl?"

"Oh, Jackie is a girl. She is almost two months old. The time sure does fly."

"Who did you marry? I don't remember Bo telling me."

"I'm not married. It's just me and Jackie."

Annie lowered her eyes, and her cheeks grew a little pink. I knew she was embarrassed, and she tried to cover it up by rearranging little Robbie's blankets. I had known the day was coming when I would have to present myself to the world as an unwed mother, and now it had arrived. I tried to gloss over my proclamation and asked about her family. After all, they had been our neighbors for years.

"So how is everyone in your family?"

"Well, of course, we're all worried about Bo. He is missing right now somewhere in France. Please pray for him!"

Her remarks about Bo unleashed an explosion of emotion that charged through my mind and my body. How could I pray for the man who had violated me and put me in a position to be looked down on by everyone? Could I pray for Bo? Could I ever forgive him for the mess he had made of my life? Could I forgive him for cheating me out of the life I could have had with the man I loved?

"Yes, Annie, I'll pray for him." *Yes, I'll pray, but not in the way you think*. My mind immediately cried out to the Lord to help me because I had a deep river of bitterness concerning Bo McAllister. I knew it was there, and I knew it was wrong, and I knew I wasn't ready to let it go.

12

Chapter

The news on the radio continued to be all bad. It seemed that Hitler was a madman who felt he could take on the whole world. The information about the Nazi death camps horrified all of us, and we lived in a constant state of fear and hopelessness. I still attended church every week, but I left Jackie home with Dad so I wouldn't call attention to myself.

I was sure that everyone in town knew about me having a baby and no husband. Leaving her home allowed me to worship with fewer awkward looks and whispers. Pastor Kirk was a wonderful man, and he encouraged me to keep coming and let God work out the rest. I was well aware that serving God was all about forgiveness. The gospel itself was Jesus forgiving us and us forgiving others. I knew the truth, but the anger I kept buried wouldn't allow the freedom I so desperately needed. I was wrestling with this issue one Sunday when I heard the lady next to me say, "Did you hear they found Bo McAllister? He's in a hospital somewhere in Europe. Poor boy—we need to pray for him!" I left church that morning with mixed emotions. I knew I had to forgive, but how?

Jackie's eyes were turning sky-blue just like Bo's. In fact, if I was perfectly honest, she looked like him more every day. I could never put him out of my mind because he was staring at me every time I picked up my baby. I knew I was coming to a breaking point. I had never told anyone who the baby's father was, not even Dad. I was so ashamed to even talk about it with anyone except the Lord. He was my only real friend. I was bottled up like a Coca-Cola, ready for the top to pop off.

I had to make a trip to the post office one Monday morning, so I asked Georgie to stay with Jackie for a few minutes. He was almost seventeen years old now and surprisingly responsible. The post office sometimes listed the casualties from our community. I always looked because my mind was always on Jack. This particular day, I was in a rush to get home, so I didn't bother looking until I heard the men behind me talking.

"It's a shame that McAllister boy died. They said he lost too much blood, and they couldn't save him. I hear the funeral is next week at the chapel on Nineteenth Street. Too many of our boys being lost!"

I waited for the men to leave and looked at the list myself. It was true—Bo was dead. I guess something broke in me at that moment. I can't explain the workings of the human heart. I just know mine broke for him and his family at that moment. In a second, all the anger and resentment flooded out of me, and I cried all the way home to Bo's little girl—the only small piece of him left.

The funeral was set for the following Friday, and many of our friends and neighbors were there. I took Jackie with me, unashamed and unafraid of what anyone thought. This was her daddy's funeral, and she needed to be there.

The service was brief, and the casket was closed. I heard talk that he was almost beyond recognition. My heart ached for his family. I gave my condolences and left quickly. I wondered if I should talk to his parents and let them know that they had a grandchild. I knew this was a difficult time for them, so I put it out of my mind for now. I prayed daily for the war to end. I was well aware that my brothers were coming to the age when they could join. Georgie talked about it all the time.

The gray days of winter moved in like a dome, keeping us

pressed down in a dark existence. Winter had always been difficult for me because I needed the sun to make me feel alive. Jackie was beginning to sit up and scoot on the floor. It was a delight to watch her explore her world.

With all the pain and heartache my family had experienced in past years, my precious baby actually brought joy in small ways to us all. We desperately needed to laugh and get our minds off of the war because there wasn't much to be happy or hopeful about. The war had brought a sense of despair that no one could escape. Everywhere you turned, people were dying. Our men were being sent home blown to pieces, and all we could do was wait and pray. The anguish and the stoic expressions on people's faces were more than I could bear.

One afternoon when Jackie was napping and Dad and the boys were gone, I went to my brothers' room, where it was quiet. I had been feeling bottled up since Bo's funeral. I knew what I needed to do, and I had put it off for weeks. The time had come when I couldn't delay any longer. This was not about Bo anymore; this was between God and me.

"God, I'm here at your feet. I know you see me, and I know you've been watching all my down sittings and my uprisings. Bo is gone, so there isn't much sense in holding a grudge toward him. For a while now, it hasn't been about him, has it?" The tears began like a trickle at first. I knew my anger and unforgivingness were not directed totally toward Bo. I had let most of that go at his funeral. I knew that back when I had let God in, I had let many things go. What I began to realize was that even when we forgive, often times we don't forget, and thoughts and attitudes can come back if we don't constantly surrender our hurt and pain to God. He always forgives us, but do we always forgive Him? I began to realize that this life with God was a daily walk, step by step. It was very much like weeding a garden—if you don't keep a constant eye, weeds can overrun your tender plants.

All of the loss that I had suffered and the trauma of the

war had caused me to develop an unhealthy attitude toward God Himself. I was that girl who had just wanted to have fun. I hadn't signed on for all the things that had happened to me. I was angry with God because He had let my mother and my little brother die and had taken Jack away from me. How could I be in such a messed-up place when I went to church every Sunday? "God, please forgive me. I give it all to you again, and this time I won't take it back." I cried long and hard, until I felt drained of all my anger and excuses.

I was not a fun-loving teenager anymore. I was a grown woman, and I had a child to raise in a time of war and without a husband. I spent a good bit of time rolling this around until finally my head cleared, and I could think. I didn't know what the future held for Jackie and me, but I did know that I had to introduce her to her grandparents and her cousin. I just didn't know how I was going to do that.

Easter was early this year, the third week of March. I loved to take Jackie shopping whenever possible. We went to town on Saturday afternoon. She was beginning to walk and wanted out of the stroller constantly. We shopped for new spring dresses to wear to church. I had been taking her every Sunday now, and she loved it. The church people seemed to overlook me and my situation. There were so many mothers there with their children and no fathers I felt accepted. People had bigger problems than gossip about their neighbors. We were at war, and everyone had a story that drew attention, so no one had time to talk about each other. We were all suffering in some way or another.

After lunch at the Hamburger Inn, we headed over to Becker's Feed Store to see the baby chicks. Kids crowded around the pen enclosed with chicken wire. The chicks were the most enchanting little creatures. They looked like small furballs, and somehow the people at the feed store had tinted their feathers. Jackie squealed with delight as the blue, red, and yellow chicks climbed over each other. I pulled her back a little from the chicken wire to calm her down. I stood up quickly and bumped right into Bo's sister Annie. "Oh, excuse me. Hi, Annie. Sorry—didn't mean to hit you. These kids are out of control!"

"Yes, I know what you mean. I'm just thankful my boy isn't old enough to want to take one home. Gracie, do you remember my mom Thelma?"

"Oh sure, I haven't seen you since the funeral. I'm so sorry about Bo. How are you doing?"

"We take it one day at a time, dear."

"Mama!" Jackie grabbed my hand because kids were pushing her out of the way. I picked her up and introduced her to Bo's sister and mother. I guess I had forgotten how much she looked like Bo, or maybe it was God's way of pushing me into making a decision that I had continued delaying. Either way, when Thelma looked into Jackie's eyes, her face went white, and she was speechless. After a few seconds, she looked at me, and I could see that she knew. She just knew.

I didn't know what to say. I knew she could read me because I was flustered and speechless myself. Kids were everywhere, and chaos was building, so I made a feeble excuse about it being Jackie's naptime and said my goodbyes.

Thelma grabbed my arm as I backed away. "Gracie, please come and see me."

I promised I would and moved away quickly. I was shaken for sure. I knew it wasn't right to keep my little girl away from her grandparents, especially since their son was dead. I knew what I had to do. Now I had to muster up enough courage to do it.

13
Chapter

Easter came and went, and spring was bursting out everywhere. I always felt brand-new when the trees bloomed and the grass turned green. Nature and the weather had always had a profound effect on me. I had been talking to God about Thelma, and I knew the time was now. I slipped Jackie into her sweater and her little saddle shoes and headed up the block to the McAllisters' home.

I was truly scared because I didn't know what to expect from these people. Even though we had been neighbors for years, I didn't know them well. They were quiet people and kept to themselves. Bo's dad spoke broken English. They had come over on the boat from Wales twenty years ago but hadn't made a lot of effort to join the social aspects of our community. They were good people, just not very social. Whenever folks were outside visiting in the neighborhood, they stayed in and never seemed interested in getting to know their neighbors. Bo had been the social butterfly of their family. With him gone, Thelma didn't go out unless Annie dragged her along.

I tapped on the screen door and waited on the back porch. Thelma slowly moved to the door to let me in.

"Hello, Thelma."

"Hello, Gracie."

Jackie squirmed in my arms to get down. She was always anxious to explore new territory.

"Gracie, would you like a cup of tea?"

"Yes, that would be wonderful."

As Thelma was preparing the tea, Jackie explored the kitchen. She kept glancing at Thelma, not sure who this woman was or how far she could go in her kitchen. Tea and cookies were served, and Jackie climbed onto my lap, looking for a cookie.

"Thelma, I know you know why I'm here today. I can't deny the resemblance between Bo and Jackie. She is Bo's daughter." I couldn't look in her eyes as tears began running down my cheeks. After several seconds, I gathered the courage to lift my head and looked into the face of a woman in pain. I could see the tears building in her eyes as she fought to keep a hold on her emotions.

"I should have come to see you sooner," I continued. "I have had a very difficult time the past couple years."

She pursed her lips and focused on Jackie, who was reaching for another cookie. After a deep sigh, she turned to me and softly spoke. "Gracie, I understand. I don't condemn you. I just want you to start at the beginning and tell me the whole story."

So that's what I did. For the next two hours I shared about my relationship with Bo, our friendship, and his betrayal. "Bo never knew about the baby. I believe he was truly sorry for what happened, and after much struggle, I forgave him. I saw Bo only one time after our night together, and I wasn't very kind to him. I was so angry with him. As I think back, I realize now he was just a teenage boy who lost control of himself and made a mistake. I am so sorry he lost his life. I owe you the biggest apology because I've denied you a chance to know your granddaughter. I know she could have been a comfort to you and your husband. I am truly sorry."

I saw tenderness in Thelma's eyes and a tinge of joy as she looked at Jackie.

"We all have struggles, honey. I am just glad that I have been able to meet this precious little girl. Bo really was a good boy, but a boy with passions and very little self-control. I believe one day he would have grown up and been a good dad to Jackie. I am sorry too that you had to go through everything alone without your mother. She was a godly woman, and I know you miss her."

"I will bring Jackie to visit you and your husband. I want her to know she has family who care about her."

Thelma reached out for Jackie, and Jackie went straight into her arms. Thelma kissed her, and Jackie patted her back just as she did my back when I hugged her. A bond had begun to form, and I was determined to keep this growing because this was the only grandmother my little girl would know.

I hugged Thelma, and she held me tight. "Gracie, you have brought joy to my heart today. Thank you."

I left Bo's home that day with a light heart. I felt as if a burden had been lifted off of my shoulders. I hadn't realized that carrying this secret for months had been like a weight holding me down. I was free now. Everyone knew about me and Jackie. Everyone except Jack.

14

Chapter

We decided to have a birthday party for Georgie. After all, a person didn't turn eighteen every day. It was a time to celebrate his coming of age. We invited everyone, including Aunt Martha, her family, and Jane. It was summer, so we cleaned up the backyard, and I draped streamers around the porch to make it look festive. People from the neighborhood started coming around noon, dropping off food and gifts.

It felt good to finally have some fun. The war had sucked all the fun from all our lives. We all needed a break from thinking about death and suffering. I knew our boys were suffering, and so were those of us who had been left behind and were trying to hold it all together. They were suffering physically, and we were suffering emotionally. The uncertainty of the times was a strain on all of us.

The party was a tremendous success. Georgie laughed so much that I thought he might crack a rib. Jane spent all her time entertaining Jackie. They became great friends. I caught up on the news with some of my old high school friends. Susie Baker told me she had heard that Jack was still in the army. He had a leg injury that had left him with a limp. He couldn't go back into combat, so they had trained him to be a medic. He was still in France, working at a hospital near the front lines.

Just the mention of his name gave my heart a jolt. I hadn't

seen Jack in three years, and yet I had the same feelings for him as if we'd been together yesterday. I could still see his eyes and feel the way I'd felt when he looked into mine. It was a look that had penetrated my heart to the core. *I'll never love anyone the way I love Jack. I have surrendered all of this to God several times. Each time I think I have it settled, someone mentions his name, and it starts all over again. Sweet Jack, why was I such a fool?*

The party began to wind down around eight, and people started strolling home. There were just a few of us left, mostly family, when Georgie stood up on the porch steps and raised his right arm. "Hey, you guys, I have an announcement to make. I signed up for the army yesterday, and I leave for basic training in two weeks! I don't want to hear all of your objections. I made the decision, and it's done. I have been wanting to do this for years, and now I'm old enough."

My heart dropped. "Georgie, why didn't you tell me?"

"Now, Gracie, I knew you would be upset and try to talk me out of it, so I kept it quiet."

"Brother, you're breaking my heart. How can you put this family through more loss and heartache?"

"Gracie, I understand, but a man has to do what he has to do. Now drop it before things are said that we both will regret."

I took Jackie and went into the house. I sat at the kitchen table and looked up as Dad came through the screen door.

"Gracie lass, your brother has to do what he feels is right for his country and for himself. You can't hold him back because of fear. He is a man now. In fact, Georgie has been a man for many years. He grew up quick in this difficult world. Pray for him and let him go."

"I don't know how much more of this war I can stand, Dad."

"We're all tired, honey, but we can't let those evil people win. We have to win, and I believe we will soon."

My dad was a source of strength for me. He was all I had to lean on for support. Georgie was not easily swayed and didn't change his mind once he'd set it. After the shock wore off from his announcement that he had enlisted, he shocked us again by bringing Mary Ann to visit. We were not aware that Georgie had a girlfriend because he had never mentioned her. He hadn't even brought her to his birthday party.

It was about dinnertime, and I was setting the table when the screen door opened, and in walked Georgie with a pretty young woman at his side.

"Gracie, I want you to meet my girlfriend, Mary Ann," he stammered awkwardly.

I was a little taken back. I had never thought of Georgie as having a romantic side. He was just my grubby little brother who worked at the junkyard.

"Well, hello. I'm Gracie, Georgie's sister."

"Pleased to meet you." She appeared shy and a little embarrassed.

"So what's for dinner, sis? I'm starved!" Georgie was always hungry. Mama had always said he would always show up at mealtime. We didn't ever need to worry about him.

"So are you both staying for dinner?"

"Yea, I figured it was about time you all met my girlfriend since we'll be getting married soon."

I could not believe what I was hearing. Dad walked in during this grand announcement, and he looked as shocked as I felt.

"Well, lad, it seems you've been busy of late. Do you think this is a rather hasty decision? After all, you'll be leaving soon. You won't have much time together."

"Dad, that's just the point. We want to spend as much time together as possible as husband and wife."

My dad had a strange look on his face, perhaps a sad longing for the time when he'd felt that way about my mother. "Where are you going to live?"

"I rented a room for a couple of weeks down on Eighteenth Street. You can rent them by the week pretty cheap. After I leave, she can go back home and stay with her family."

Mary Ann looked at the floor, glancing from time to time

at Georgie. She was young and in love and the perfect picture of a blushing bride.

"Young lady, what do you think?" Dad asked his soon-to-be daughter-in-law.

"Mr. McDonald," she started slowly, "I love Georgie, and nothing would make me happier than to be his wife. I think it will be easier on him if he knows I'm waiting here at home for him."

When she said that, my throat tightened. She was giving her man some hope, something to cling to when he was scared and lonely, exactly what I hadn't given—or couldn't give—Jack. Instead, I had given him hurt, rejection, and a sense of hopelessness to carry with him into war. Guilt rose in my chest, and tears stung my eyes.

Georgie shot me a look. "Gracie, you don't have to cry about it. Everybody gets married sooner or later. Sheesh!"

Georgie didn't know about me and Jack and how we'd parted. My little brothers had never asked me about Jackie's father. They had never been critical of me or my little girl. I guess I was blessed that they just loved us and went about their own lives. We were all accepting and independent, willing to live and let live.

"I *am* happy for you, just surprised. Sit down now and tell us your plans!"

Later, when I was in bed, I cried hard for all the bad decisions I had made. How would I ever get another chance to love Jack and make up for all the hurt I had caused him?

Georgie and Mary Ann got married two days later at the courthouse. No one came to the wedding except Dad and me as witnesses. Mary Ann came from a large Irish family that lived across the river, and no one had transportation to the city. She had six young brothers and one sister who kept her mother busy. Georgie and Mary Ann had met at the roller rink in town. She was only seventeen years old, and they'd liked each other right from the start. They had arranged to meet every weekend for months. When Georgie decided to enlist, he popped the question. Her parents had so many kids that it had never occurred to them that she was falling in love. They had given her their blessing when she told them, and that was that.

Young couples were getting married quickly during the war. They knew that separation was inevitable, so many grabbed the chance to love and be loved while it was possible. It was a time of impulsive decisions made in the heat of passion, discounting common sense. Throughout history, women had sent their men off to war, promising to love them and wait for their return. Unfortunately, I was not one of those women. Georgie and his bride spent their honeymoon alone. They came to dinner a few times, but we could all tell they just wanted to be alone. It was heartwarming and precious to watch them together. Young love was a gift from God.

Georgie left two weeks later. I cried and hugged him. "You behave yourself," I teased him, with tears on my cheeks.

He was a tough kid, and I came to the realization that if anyone could get through this war unscathed, it would be Georgie. Mary Ann went home and promised she would find a way to visit.

We settled back into a routine. Dad went to work, and Sammy by now had established himself as the town pool champion. Dad had quit trying to keep him out of the pool hall. It was his calling, and he took to it like a fish to water. He spent most days and nights shooting pool. He challenged all comers and usually came out the victor. It was not the life we would have chosen for Sammy, but it was the life he'd wanted from the time he started shooting marbles on our front sidewalk. He made a pretty good living and had fun doing it. There was no way he would ever join the army. He'd had a heart murmur from birth, so he would never pass the physical. He had no desire to serve anyway. Sammy was a good-time Charlie. He was out to have fun, and he could entertain people for hours.

He had found his calling, and I was just happy he would stay home from the war.

I took Jackie to visit the McAllister family as often as I could, and Annie would bring her little boy by to play. It was a special time, watching my little girl grow and interact with other children. She didn't have a daddy like other kids, but she had two grandpas and a grandma who loved her and spent time with her. I was beginning to be thankful for what I had instead of pining for things I didn't. Concentrating on what I didn't have always led me back to all the loss I had suffered. I couldn't live in the past anymore. I kept my mind on the future. I could be in control and powerful or weak and pitiful; it was my choice. During this period in my life, I was learning about myself and who I was and what I wanted. I guess you could say that I was growing up and learning about choices. I read a poem that spoke volumes to me one afternoon. I felt as if the author was speaking about my life.

"Invictus" by William Ernest Henley

> Out of the night that covers me,
> Black as the pit from pole to pole,
> I thank whatever gods may be
> For my unconquerable soul.
>
> In the fell clutch of circumstance
> I have not winced nor cried aloud.
> Under the bludgeoning of chance
> My head is bloody, but unbowed.
>
> Beyond this place of wrath and tears
> Looms but Horror of the shade,
> And yet the menace of the years

Finds and shell find me unafraid.
It matters not how strait the gate,
How charged with punishment the scroll,
I am master of my fate I am the captain of my
soul.

I was in charge of my life now, and the choices I made, I had to live with. God was giving me the wisdom I needed to make wise choices, but I had to make them. Before, my life had always been about me and having fun. I hadn't wanted responsibility and commitment. Since I had learned to commit to the Lord now, I was ready to commit to the life He had for me. I was not the same person I once had been. I looked at life from a whole new perspective. God was getting me ready for something, I could feel it. I took one day at a time and didn't rush through life at top speed. I could wait on God because He had waited on me.

15

Chapter

It was 1944, and the war continued. I had begun working at the soda fountain on Saturdays, and Dad watched Jackie for me. It felt good to get out of the house and see people and do something for myself. I liked the people I worked with. They always had funny stories about the customers that kept me in stitches. They say laughter is healing for the soul, and my soul needed it, just like the souls of everyone else in our country.

Bo's sister Annie and I had so much in common that we became great friends. She had her little boy Robert, and I had Jackie. Her husband was serving in the Philippines. We took the kids to the park for a picnic one afternoon, to let them run off some of that energy that small children seemed to manufacture. I was packing up the leftover snacks when I looked up directly into the face of Jack's sister Betsey. I was taken off guard for a moment. It had been years since I had seen either of his sisters.

She stopped dead in her tracks and looked me straight in the eyes. "Well, what a surprise to see you, Gracie. It's been a while."

"Hello, Betsey. It has been a while. How is your family?"

"Dad and Mom are fine, working hard with the war effort, as everyone is."

A tall, thin young man walked toward us, smiling. "Hey, Betz, who's your friend?"

"Oh, she isn't my friend. This is the girl that broke my brother's heart," she said curtly. She turned back to me. "This is my boyfriend Roy."

For a moment, I was too shocked by her comment to speak. I couldn't deny that I was the girl who had broken Jack's heart and probably led him to sign up to fight. I was probably responsible for him getting wounded too. Everything was my fault. Just as I was standing up and trying to find my next word, Jackie came running toward me, screaming, "Mama, look! I found a caterpillar in the grass. Isn't it beautiful?"

Betsey looked from Jackie to me with shock and contempt. "So, Gracie, is this your little girl?"

I pulled Jackie into my arms and looked at her treasure. "Ah, it is a fine caterpillar. Yes, this is my daughter, Jackie."

"Pleased to meet you, ma'am." Jackie smiled in her sweet way, took her woolly worm, and skipped off to play with Robert.

Betsey glared at me with fire shooting from her eyes. "Where is Jackie's daddy? How could you name her Jackie? You are despicable."

I knew I needed to say something. The old Gracie would not have let her get away with her insults, but I was not the same person that I once had been. "I'm sorry, Betsey, for all the grief I caused Jack and your family."

"Well, sorry doesn't nearly cover it. I hope you get everything you deserve. Come on, Roy. I need some fresh air. It stinks around here."

Betsey and her friend walked off, and I sat back down, trying to choke back the hurt and sobs that were stuck in my throat. The old feelings began to swirl around in my head. Thoughts were exploding in my brain like bombs in a minefield. I was sure Betsey would race home and tell her parents all about me and my child named Jackie. *What will they think? Will they all sit around their beautiful hand-finished table and condemn me? Will they write Jack and tell him I have a child?* I felt as if my lunch was coming back up on the waves of guilt and shame.

God, I need you now. Please help me. In my spirit I felt like God was with me, and after a few minutes I managed to swallow the hurt and shock.

We had learned in church a few weeks ago that God never condemns us, and we shouldn't condemn ourselves. I understood it and believed it, but when someone stood up and condemned you to your face, it was hard to ignore. If only Betsey knew the pain her words had caused. It would have been easier if she would have slapped me in the face.

I was working at the soda bar on Saturday, washing glasses, when I felt someone staring at me. I looked up, and there in front of me stood Betsey and her mother Mildred.

Mildred spoke first. "Gracie, could we have a word with you?"

"Um, sure … give me a minute to get someone to cover for me."

We found a quiet corner in which to talk as anxiety tried to overcome me.

"I just have one question for you, Gracie. Does your little girl belong to Jack? Have you kept my grandchild from me all these years?"

I tried to speak, but words would not come out. This woman had always been someone who demanded her way, and she usually got it. She was arrogant and haughty with little concern for anyone besides herself and her family. She had never cared for me. She had felt that I was not good enough for her son and had discouraged our relationship the whole time we were together. Now she stood in front of me, demanding to know who my precious Jackie's father was. I had never told anyone who had fathered my baby except Bo's family and Dad. This woman had no right to question me about my child. With this family's second attempt to humiliate me, something broke in me. I was strong-willed, and even though I had mellowed out, I still had a temper that, if unleashed, could run havoc. I gained control of myself and simply said, "This child is my child, not Jack's, and anything else concerning her is none of your business. Now kindly leave my place of employment."

Mildred appeared shocked, and if truth be known, I had even shocked myself. The calm, decisive way I had answered her showed more strength than I had. I had never thought I was capable of standing up to people like her, but no one was going to hurt my little girl, ever!

I could only imagine what these women would write to Jack. I was not sure if he could receive mail now. I thought and prayed about this for weeks until a plan began to form in my mind.

16

Chapter

Things were beginning to move in our favor in the war effort. Thousands of British, American, and Canadian forces landed on the beaches in Normandy off the coast of France. This landing covered fifty miles of beach and was the largest military assault in history. We were beginning to win, and that meant our boys would be coming home. This operation was called D-Day, and it would come to be known as the beginning of the end of our war in Europe. We were all hopeful as we sat glued to our radios. This war had gone on too long, and weariness showed in all of our lives.

I didn't know where Jack was now or what shape he was in, but I decided to write to him so that he at least would get the truth. I had no right to expect anything from him. We hadn't seen each other in years. He might have forgotten all about me. But I wanted to explain and ask for his forgiveness for hurting him the way I had. I knew it was going to be a difficult letter to write. I spent a week just thinking and trying to put my thoughts in order. I decided to just tell him the truth, the whole story. I didn't know exactly how to get his address, so I started at the post office. Much to my surprise, they had a list of all the servicemen from our community and where they were right now. Jack's name was about midway down the list. He was still in France, working at a military hospital. I now was emotionally ready to write this letter, so I began.

> *Dear Jack,*
>
> *I'm not sure this letter will ever reach you, but I am taking a chance that it will. I have a lot to explain, and I feel the time is now. I saw your mother and sister Betsey the other day. Perhaps they wrote to you about it. I think your family has a bad opinion of me, so I would like to clear things up.*
>
> *First, I want to tell you that I have a little girl. She is four years old. I also need to say that I am not married. Her father made a bad choice, which created an unexpected pregnancy. He died in the war, and I'm raising her on my own with my dad's help even though it has been tough. I love her, and she is not a mistake. I wanted you to know the truth. You are the only man I have ever loved, and I will love you till the day I die. I am sorry for all the hurt that I've caused you. I'm sorry I wasn't ready for the life you offered me. I regret that decision every day of my life. I hope you are well. I pray every day that this war will end, and all of our boys will come home.*
>
> *I hope you will talk to me someday. Even if you don't want to, I wish you well and the very best life possible.*
>
> *Always,*
> *Gracie*

I addressed the letter and took it to the post office quickly, before I could change my mind. I felt sick to my stomach, thinking that Jack hated me. I had no way of knowing what his family had said about me or what rumors he had heard, but I wanted him to know the truth. I had read in my Bible the other night that if you knew the truth, it would set you free. I needed to be free, and so did he.

I woke up early with a cramp in my foot. I jumped out of bed and walked it off. Jackie was still asleep, so I slipped downstairs to put some coffee on for Dad before he went to work. It was going to be another hot August day. The summer had been hot and humid, and our house seemed to heat up early in the morning. All the windows were open, and we had a fan, but it just blew the hot air around. I had been filling a washtub with cool water in the afternoons and letting Jackie play in it to cool her off. I turned on the radio to get the news and the weather report. It was going to be another hot day with no chance of relief until the weekend. I switched to some music and started breakfast. I heard Dad moving upstairs, getting ready for work. Jackie came slowly down the steps and straight to me for a hug. She had trouble waking up in the morning, so cuddle time was a necessary start to her day. I got breakfast on the table, and we all sat down and tried to eat in spite of the staggering heat.

Sammy came in to join us. "They say this war can't go on much longer," Sammy said. "D-Day has shut Germany down. It's those Japs that won't give up." Dad looked up from his plate and thanked God that Georgie had never left the States. He was in Arkansas, training troops. It had turned out that Georgie was a great drill instructor, so he spent his time training the recruits and never had to go to the front. God answered so many of my prayers during the war. I had begun to write down all the answers so I could remember them. The answer to one prayer had not materialized yet. I wanted to see Jack one more time, even if it was the last time.

As we were finishing breakfast, the music on the radio stopped for an important announcement. We all stiffened and listened intently. The announcer said that the president had released a statement to the press, which read: "Sixteen hours ago, an American plane dropped a bomb on Hiroshima, Japan, to destroy their capability to continue this war." If this did not stop Japan, the announcer continued, the United States would rain bombs until they gave in. We were stunned. We would not know until much later the magnitude of that bomb. We sat looking at one another, not knowing what this meant. We knew the war in Europe was about finished, but the Japanese had been relentless in their efforts to destroy us. Little did we know that at that moment the war was over; Japan surrendered a month later.

As time passed and the reality of the war ending settled in, celebrations began breaking out across the nation. Our boys were coming home! Families would be reunited, and kids could see their dads again or maybe even meet them for the first time. It was a time of great joy but sadness too. There were many coming home without limbs or eyes. There were men who appeared to be the same physically but who were forever changed emotionally and mentally.

My friend Annie's husband was one of the first to arrive home. I rejoiced with her when we found out his ship would dock in New York, and he would board a train to reach Indiana. Annie was beside herself with excitement. He arrived in mid-afternoon, and we were all waiting. When he climbed down the steps of the train, he appeared a little disoriented. Annie gathered him in her arms, overcome with emotion. He didn't wrap his arms around her at first. He stood still and weak. She pulled away and looked deep into his eyes. He didn't seem to know who she was at first, but after he looked at her for a minute, he began to weep, softly at first, and then he pulled her to him and sobbed.

It broke my heart to watch this unfold. I suddenly understood why people said war was the most destructive of all human activities. I had already understood the physical pain and suffering. I knew that if someone lost a leg or an arm, they would need help and care the rest of their lives. I guess what I hadn't understood was the pain and torment of being separated from those you love, the lack of connection and touch that all humans need. It seemed inhumane to separate people from their loved ones for long periods of time. Isolation and loneliness were cancers that ate away at the soul. I wanted to believe that time would heal, but I knew in my heart that only the hand of God Almighty could heal the casualties of this war.

Sons, fathers, and husbands began coming home in droves. It seemed like trains were steaming in around the clock. Dad said he filled up with tears every day as he watched families being reunited. Many of the young men from my neighborhood could be seen walking down the street holding their kids and their wives, all of them clinging to each other.

It was a special time for families, filled with joy and heartache. One family on my street lost two sons in the war. The first of Mr. and Mrs. Keenan's boys had been killed in the beginning at Pearl Harbor. They had tried to hold the other son, Bobby, back, but he wouldn't stay. He felt he needed to fight back for what they'd done to his brother.

Susie Kline, the postmaster, had lost her only son. He had been killed when they stormed the beaches at Normandy. She had a daughter and two grandchildren to help soothe her pain. She told me one day that she would never get over losing her boy. I understood because I remembered when Mama lost Kenny. She had never really been the same after that. The stories never ended, and the mixture of pain and joy continued. We had to heal the best way we could if we were going to go on living.

17
Chapter

I dreamed about Jack one night. I dreamed he had come home and was looking for me. He was wandering through the woods on the creek bank where we used to meet in high school. He kept looking and calling my name, but he never found me. I woke up crying and feeling a sense of loss. This dream bothered me for weeks. I felt as if Jack had died somehow, and I would never see him again. No one I had contact with knew anything about Jack and his return. I had never received an answer to the letter I'd written him; I was not even sure he'd gotten it. Every time I thought about him, my heart hurt. I still loved him. He was my first and only love. Somehow God would help me overcome this hole in my heart, but only He knew how.

Mable McTavish agreed to care for Jackie a couple of days each week so I could work more. I was feeling bad about depending on Dad for our livelihood. She was growing up and soon would go to school. Mable worked cheap, so we struck a deal. I worked three days a week, and they moved me to the housewares department at Woolworth's. It seemed this was a busy place because of families getting their lives back on track and setting up households together. Many wives and children had been living with parents, and now they were finding their own homes.

I enjoyed working, and Jackie loved being at Mable's house.

Mable's granddaughter stayed with her too, so they could entertain each other. Since the war ended, it seemed as if our population had grown. Our downtown was flooded with people day and night. The clubs at night were full of people celebrating and reuniting with old friends. I didn't attend those celebrations. I had lost my interest in dancing and that kind of social life. I just wanted to work and care for Jackie. She was my whole life now. All in all, I was a good mother, probably because I'd had the perfect mother. I believed that she was in heaven cheering me on, and that gave me a sense of peaceful assurance that things would be okay.

It was Saturday, and the city had a huge parade planned to celebrate the homecoming of our troops. It was to be a military parade, and all those who had served were to march. I was working that day, but we were allowed to watch the parade as it went by our store. The atmosphere was electric with excitement. I felt such a tremendous sense of pride rise in me. Our young men and women had stood up and fought to bring down an evil regime that was threatening the whole world. I yelled out the words "God Bless America" with all the strength I could muster.

There were so many men in uniform from every branch of service. It warmed my heart to see them so proud of what they had accomplished. I looked closely at one group of regular army to see if I knew any of them. I thought I recognized a couple of the soldiers, and then I saw what made my heart stop. Marching down the street directly in front of me was Jack. I would know him anywhere with his strong jaw and straight back, pulled up to his full six feet. As he walked by, I saw the slight limp, and I couldn't hold back the tears that flowed down my face. Jack was alive and home, but he hadn't come home to me. He didn't belong to me. I felt an unbearable sadness settle over me.

I fought hard to put Jack out of my mind. Seeing him again stirred up all the old feelings and regrets, but I had to go on and make a life for myself and my child. I knew in my head that what I was thinking was right, but how could I make my heart line up with my head?

Annie, Bo's sister, was probably my best friend at this time in my life. It was funny how Bo's family had become like family to me. Annie and I took the kids to the playground in the evenings so they could play, and we could talk. Robbie was trying desperately to find a job. Since he'd come home, they had been trying to get their lives back on track. They were living with Annie's folks, which made things more difficult. The kids were happily engaged on the merry-go-round, so I took the opportunity to stick my nose into her business just a little. "Annie, are ye sick or something? You look so tired and sad."

"No, I'm okay," she said quickly.

"I thought you'd be over the top with happiness since Robbie came home."

She looked like a sky with storm clouds forming. She was definitely clouding up to rain. The tears started slowly and then began to pour.

"Annie, sweetheart, what's wrong?"

I waited while the tears slowed and she got control of herself.

"I don't want to burden you with my problems, Gracie."

"Annie, you are my best friend, the closest thing I have to a sister. I want to help any way I can."

She reluctantly began to share what she had been holding inside. Once she started, it all came tumbling out in waves. "It's Robbie. He has been having trouble sleeping at night. He wakes up crying or shouting out in his sleep. He feels bad waking me up but can't seem to stop. He worries all the time about everything. This job business is getting to him constantly. If he comes home with another denial, it puts him in a mood that nothing can get through. Some evenings he sits and looks off into space and won't talk to anyone. He's nervous and scared to go anywhere or associate with people. I just don't get it. He wasn't wounded in the war; it just scared him, I guess."

"I am so sorry, Annie. I guess being away from home in

a horrible situation does things to people." I hugged her and promised to pray for them.

Going forward, I tried to help out with little Robert as much as possible. I would bring him to our house to play with Jackie to take some of the pressure off of Annie. It was tragic to see what war had done to Robbie and thousands of others. We were all thankful that the war was over, but everyone was struggling to put the pieces of their lives back together.

One Sunday morning, Annie called me very early to ask if I would take Robert to church with us. Robbie had had a bad night, and she wanted to stay home with him. I was happy to help, so Jackie and I stopped for Robert on our way. We always walked the three blocks to church, and as the three of us walked, we chatted as usual. Robert was a very intelligent boy and very verbal. He was always talking on and on about something. It was no surprise when he began talking about his dad.

"Miss Gracie, why do you think my dad yells at me so much?"

"I don't know, Robert. What do you mean?"

"Last night he was just sitting in his chair, and I asked him why he was so sad. He pushed me away and yelled really loud to leave him alone. Why won't my daddy play with me? Why is he mad at me?"

My heart broke for this little boy. How could children be expected to understand something that adults didn't understand?

"Robert, your daddy isn't mad at you. This has nothing to do with you. He's mad at the war, and it makes him sad to think about it. When he's sitting in his chair, he's thinking about the war and all the scary things that happened. It's hard for him to forget."

"Miss Gracie, but why does he yell at me? I wasn't at the war."

I had no answer for this question. "I didn't know, honey. I only know your daddy loves you, and he doesn't want to yell.

He just can't help it. It seems to me when someone gets hurt inside them, it's hard to push it out. It wants to stay there and keep on hurting them."

As we continued to walk, I asked God to give me some answers for this sad, sweet little boy.

"Robert, we're going to pray for your mommy and daddy today at church." I knew only God could heal this man and rescue this family.

After church I took the kids home and made lunch. They played well together, and it warmed my heart that Jackie had a friend. I spent a lot of time thinking about how Jackie was growing up without a father. She had asked me several times about her daddy. I had explained briefly that he had been killed in the war. That seemed to be enough to satisfy her for now. She was growing up, and I didn't know how long I had before she would want more in-depth answers that I wasn't prepared to give.

Dad came in from the backyard and asked the kids if they wanted to take a walk with him. "Gracie, you look tired. Take a nap, and I'll play with these kiddos for a while." My father was so good to me. Never had he lost his temper or condemned me for being a single woman raising a child on her own. We worked together to make our lives manageable.

"Come on, you little squirts. Let's give this lady some time to rest and see if we can find an ice cream cone somewhere."

The kids shrieked with delight and left with Dad.

It was so nice to have the house quiet, and I settled down on the couch and drifted off, thinking only of Jack. Whenever I had some quiet time, his face always came to my mind. I could still see him marching down Market Street with his gun over his shoulder, looking straight ahead. I didn't think about him when I was busy, but in these quiet times, I could think of no one but him. I woke suddenly when I heard pounding on the door. I jumped up, startled, and opened the door. Annie was standing there out of breath, her face wet with tears.

"Annie, what's wrong?"

"We're taking Robbie to the hospital! Gracie, he tried to cut his wrists! He says he wants to die. I don't know what I'm going to do."

I put my arms around her and tried to calm her down.

"I've got to go," she said. "Can you please keep Robert for me?"

"Yes, don't worry about him!"

I prayed and prayed all day and evening for Annie and Robbie. We all thought the war was over, but for some it had just begun. Annie came by the next morning. She was worn to a frazzle but wanted to take Robert home. Robbie was in the hospital and would stay there for some time. He had had a nervous breakdown and would require medicine and counseling. Apparently, many of the soldiers coming home were dealing with this same thing. The government had established the GI Bill of Rights for returning veterans, which helped families get medical treatment for physical and mental disorders. This bill helped men to get retrained so they could get jobs and even helped families get loans to buy homes. The government knew its people had sacrificed greatly, and now it was time to help people heal.

18

Chapter

Mary Ann came to visit one Sunday afternoon. We hadn't seen much of her since Georgie left. He hadn't written to us much, just a short note now and then. Our news about him or his wife was scarce. She was living with her family across the river, so it was difficult to visit. The bus would bring her to downtown, and then she had to walk to our neighborhood. I liked Mary Ann. She was quiet, unlike me, but we complemented each other well.

I heard the knock on the front door and hurried to open it. There on the front stoop was Mary Ann. She smiled and said, "Hi, Gracie. It's so nice to see you." She had a lovely smile, and just looking at her warmed your heart.

"Mary Ann, so nice to see you," I said.

As she stepped through the door, my eyes moved from her face to the bulge in her middle.

"Mary Ann, you're expecting!"

"Yes, I'm six months along. Didn't Georgie tell you?"

"No, that boy never tells us anything! How are you feeling?"

"I'm great. No problems at all. My mother has birthed so many children that it's second nature to me."

"Dad, look who's here, and look at what she brought with her."

"Mary Ann, how nice to see you. Well, I'll be—there's a wee one on the way!"

"Hello, Grandpa!" Mary Ann said with a twinkle in her eye.

"Yes, I guess that's going to be my new name. What a pleasant surprise. Georgie never said a word to us."

"He says he's pretty busy down there, but it's all going to change since the war ended. He's due to be discharged in about two months. He should be home right before the baby arrives."

"Where are you two going to live?" Dad seemed very interested in where and what they would be doing after Georgie came home. He was always concerned about how we all would make a living and have a place to live. I figured it must stem from his need to take care of his family.

"We're not sure yet. I am asking around to see if there are any houses for rent. We'd love to stay on this side of the river so Georgie can get a good job. Have you heard of any houses for rent around here? We'd like to be close to family."

"Not to my knowledge, sweetheart, but Gracie and I will start looking."

We spent a pleasant afternoon with Mary Ann. Georgie sure had picked a good woman. Maybe the boy had more sense than I'd ever given him credit for all these years. Mama had always said not to worry about Georgie, that he could take care of himself, and I had begun to believe she was right. I was so excited to think about an addition to our family. I had always been someone who loved people, especially family. Pastor Kirk had told me one time that I had a gift of hospitality. He never missed an opportunity to see the good in people. He always saw good in me when I could see nothing but bad. When you left his church, you felt as if there was hope for you. You could walk into his church on a rainy day and walk out feeling like the sun had broken through even if it was still raining.

I spent many nights praying for my brothers and my dad. They still hadn't come back to church. I knew my dad's heart was still broken over my mum. My brothers were a work in progress, trying to figure out their lives in a world that was spinning so fast that all most of us could do was hold on with both hands.

Mary Ann came from a Christian family. She told me her mother was a godly woman. Her dad was a plumber, and they lived on the edge of town. The family grew their own food because of so many mouths to feed. She was one of two girls and had five younger brothers and one older. Her older brother worked with her dad, but the other four boys were under twelve, and her sister was in her teens. Mary Ann was her mother's helper with the housework and with tending to the younger kids. I sometimes wondered if she'd wanted to get married just to get away from all the demands that were made on her. I was sure she loved Georgie, and I prayed everything would work out, but so many young people were making impulsive decisions that turned out to be bad decisions.

I seemed to be taking on the role of the person praying for the family. I didn't know why. I just carried so many people in my heart and wanted the best for them. I set up a meeting with Pastor Kirk one Sunday afternoon. I tried to explain the feelings I had for my family and friends. Annie and her husband were still struggling. Robbie was home again now and still looking for work. Annie said the GI Bill was going to help him get some training. I hurt so much for them. They were good people, and Robbie had made a tremendous sacrifice for our country. He and so many other soldiers were trying to figure out what to do next.

The pastor invited me into his little office, the same little office where I'd felt God take away all my anger and grief that day years ago. God had saved me that day from a life of regret and torment.

"Gracie, would you like a cup of tea?"

"Yes, thank you so much."

"You've been a busy girl, I hear. You're working and caring for your family, ah?"

"Yes, I'm working five days a week at Woolworth's. I really

like my job. They have made me a manager in the home goods department. Our little town is really growing, Pastor. Some days there are so many people in our store, I can barely get a lunch break."

"Ah, I only wish those same folks were flocking to church like they are to shopping. I see so many young folks who have time for everything but God. It saddens my heart."

"It's funny you brought that up. That's the very reason I'm here. I have such concern for my family and neighbors. I sometimes hurt for them so much. What can I do besides pray?"

"Lass, you're what we call an intercessor, someone who makes prayers for others. It seems God just keeps revealing the special gifts He has for you. Do you think He is trying show you just how valuable you are to Him? Lass, I don't know if you know this or not, but your mum was just like you. She was constantly praying for people. She would give me a list some days to pray for certain people. Gracie, your mama was a rare woman far beyond how you knew her."

I hadn't known anything about her praying for people. I was so busy trying to have fun and live my own life that I'd never considered anyone else but myself. "I bet she prayed for me every day."

"Yes, I think she did pray for you and your whole family."

"Pastor, you know I'm raising my daughter without a father. I sometimes worry about her and all the questions she's going to ask someday. What can I tell her?"

"Lass, just pray, answer her questions, and leave it with the good Lord. He will show you what to say in due time. Gracie, God has all of the answers. Don't carry the weight of it yourself. Take one day at a time and rest in Him."

After a talk with Pastor Kirk, I always felt renewed. He had a way about him that brought peace to my heart and mind. I had so many people in my life who helped me. I guessed it was because my Mum had prayed for them and me long before she left.

19

Chapter

New businesses were beginning to open all over town. People were rebuilding their lives and their homes. It was a very exciting time. My new job as manager of housewares brought more responsibilities. I was good at it because I had managed my dad's household for years, and I wasn't afraid of people. I could strike up a conversation with anyone. New household appliances were coming on the market monthly, and everyone wanted the new gadgets. Sunbeam had developed a toaster that would drop the bread down to a coil, and then when the bread was toasted, you could pull it up. We couldn't keep them in the store; they sold like hotcakes. We took pride in stocking the most popular items on the market. I loved my job because it made me feel important. I liked succeeding because for so long I had felt like a failure. It was amazing how some success had a way of healing your opinion of yourself.

At this point in my life, I met Billy Frye. Billy was the manager of the whole store. He was brought in from Virginia to get our store in shape. We were growing rapidly and needed to be restructured. Billy had a lot of experience. He had been in retail for ten years and had gotten other stores organized and running smoothly. He was about five years older than me, and we hit it off right from the beginning. I think it was Billy's dry sense of humor that first attracted me to him. He made me laugh, and I had always liked people who made me laugh. Some days there was chaos in our store, but Billy always kept a cool head. He calmly smoothed over issues, and people left smiling and thanking him for his help.

One afternoon a customer brought back a whole set of dishes that she claimed were broken when she opened the box. Billy spoke calmly, as usual. "Ma'am, are you sure you didn't drop these dishes somewhere along the way going home?"

"No, sir, I was very careful all the way home."

"We certainly want to make this right. Do you have your sales receipt?"

The lady was not listening at the time because her little boy was pulling silverware off of the counter behind her. "Teddy, get over here before you break something else!"

Billy picked up on that right away. "Hi, Teddy. How are you today?"

"I'm fine."

"Mom said you broke something before. What was that?"

"Oh, those dishes she brought back. I climbed on the box at home, and we heard them break. Boy, was she mad."

Billy turned to the startled customer and said, "Sorry, ma'am. We cannot take back merchandise that was damaged at home."

Billy was good at his job, and we all loved him. I guess that's why I decided to accept his offer for dinner when he asked me out a couple of weeks later. I hadn't been on a date for years. I don't know if that was because of Bo or my loyalty to Jack. I had put that part of my life aside in order to care for Jackie. Jack still held my heart even if he never wanted to see me again; he would always hold my heart in his hands. On an impulse I accepted Billy's offer.

On Saturday after the store closed, Billy and I headed out to Burette's, a small Italian restaurant just four blocks down the street from our store. I had arranged for Dad to watch Jackie. He agreed that I needed some adult conversation. He worried that I was alone and never having any fun. "Gracie, it's not normal for a lass to not have any friends," he had said. "You need to meet people your own age. You might find ye a husband."

Billy was easy to talk to, and before long I was relaxing and truly enjoying myself. He had never been married, even though most young people our age had been married a few years by now. He had been raised on a farm in rural Richmond, Virginia. He had missed the war because he was his mother's only son and her sole support. His dad had died when he was a senior in high school. Billy's mother had moved in with her sister when work started moving Billy around from place to place.

"I guess the reason I never got married was I never had time to get serious with anyone. I'd meet someone and start a relationship, and boom, they'd move me again. Don't get me wrong—I like traveling and meeting new people, but it gets kind of lonely, never having anyone to come home to. I hope someday to find a store that I can make my home base and maybe get married and start a family."

Billy knew I had a daughter, but I didn't share my personal story with him. He probably just assumed her daddy had been killed in the war, which was technically the truth. All in all, it was a pleasant evening, and I appreciated his friendship.

I was slowly beginning to realize that Jack was never going to get in touch with me. I didn't know if he had gotten my letter. I was positive his family had done everything possible to turn him against me. I could not even imagine what was going on in his mind concerning me. I so wanted to see him and explain myself. We lived in different parts of town, so it was unlikely I would run into him in my neighborhood. I prayed for his forgiveness. I knew God had forgiven me, but I also understood that God's forgiveness did not necessarily bring about man's forgiveness.

Carole Marvin

Across the street from Woolworth's, a renovation was beginning on an abandoned building. Everyone was always curious about any new businesses moving into downtown. I was out for lunch one afternoon and saw carpenters knocking down walls and enlarging the building. It didn't look like an all-purpose store like ours. I was hoping we wouldn't have competition. Our store sold everything from car tires to baby clothes. Anything you wanted could be purchased. Our store slogan was "If we don't have it, they don't make it." Our soda bar had been modernized too. We now had a full lunch counter that served lunch and breakfast. I was proud to work at one of the most favored stores in town. If someone believed they could compete with us, they would be unpleasantly surprised.

I arrived to work early one Tuesday morning. I had some inventory I needed to finish. I always walked to work and enjoyed the fresh air. It also kept me in shape. My body and my life were taking shape, and I felt good about myself. As I hurried to the store, I glanced across the street to the newly renovated building. I saw a sign leaning against the outside wall. Men were preparing to hoist it up to the front of the building. I tried to read what it said but couldn't quite make it out.

I hurried on into the store to prepare for the rush and finish my paperwork. We were having a sale on bedsheets today, and the price was ridiculously low, so I knew we'd be busy. Soon the customers swarmed in, and once again, I had no break. I ate lunch on the run and never stopped until five o'clock, when we closed the doors. Exhausted, I gathered up my purse and headed out the door. I just wanted to go home, put my feet up, and have a cup of coffee. As I started down the block, I glanced once again across the street and saw the sign had been hung. It was large with green lettering: TOM WILSON AND SON FURNITURE. Jack! Jack was Tom Wilson's son!

I continued walking home, but the shock of seeing that sign blinded me to everything around me. Afterward I didn't remember crossing streets or seeing people. All I could see was that sign. It was like a stoplight flashing in my brain. Questions were assaulting my mind: Would Jack be working directly across the street from me every day? Every time I walked out of my store, would I risk seeing him? Would he come to our lunch counter for lunch and sit down next to me? My mind whirled like a spinning wheel. I wanted to see Jack, and yet I didn't want to see him. I wanted to explain myself in person about Jackie and everything that had happened with Bo, and yet I didn't want to humiliate myself and see the contempt in his eyes. *God, please help me!*

I used to get up every morning looking forward to starting my day. I loved walking to work even when the air started getting chilly. It seemed I could breathe freely and share my innermost thoughts with the Lord. It was a time of communion between me and my best friend. I talked to Him, and I believed He talked to me. Those times had been precious, but now that feeling was gone. I didn't want to get out of bed in the morning. I dreaded walking into town because I had a horrible fear that I was going to come face-to-face with Jack. He would never again look at me the way he once had. The love that had shone from his eyes to mine was gone forever, and I'd never see it again. I was no longer his beautiful brown-eyed girl. I couldn't bear to see the disappointment in his eyes. The intimacy we once had shared was gone, washed away by the pain and heartache that I had created. No, Jack didn't want to ever see me again. I prayed every morning going forward that our paths would never cross.

20

Chapter

Winter was moving in quickly, bringing early snow and sleet. Christmas was approaching, and I tried to shop for Jackie on my lunch breaks. Billy gave me a ride home whenever the weather was fierce. We were good friends, and my affection for him was growing. We went out to dinner occasionally, but it was not a romantic relationship for me. I had only one man in my heart, and I had lost him. Billy did mention one night that he would like to make Evansville his home base. He was sick of being moved all the time. Billy was a sincerely good guy. He had a heart of gold, and I knew he would do anything for me. If I needed something at the store, he was by my side in an instant. I so appreciated the rides home after work because the snow and cold were intensifying. I invited him to stay for dinner a few times.

Dad liked Billy, and they teased each other. "Say, Billy boy, do you think those Cleveland Indians will get a new hitter this season, or do they like losing all the time?"

"Well, I really don't know, Willie, but the Pittsburgh Pirates can't seem to find anyone who can catch the ball. The game involves hitting and catching, right?"

They would laugh and tease each other, and after a few games of checkers, Billy would head home. It was amazing how well they got along. I hadn't seen my dad laugh much since

Mama died, so I appreciated any and all laughter. Mama used to say laughter was good for the soul, and I was witnessing it firsthand.

Jackie would climb on Billy's lap any chance she got and pull on his ears and nose. He called her a wiggle worm. As soon as he walked in the door, she was at his side. It saddened me to realize how much she needed male attention; she needed a dad. Billy attempted to teach Jackie to play checkers. Some evenings it was a fruitless effort. She understood the basic concept of the game but refused to take it seriously. She would rather tease him and act silly.

"Jackie, you got yourself a king—put a checker on top of the other."

"No, I don't want a king. I want a princess. Please, Billy, can I have a princess?"

"No, it's called a king. A king is better than a princess."

"I'm a girl. I can't be a king. I want to be a princess!"

This would go on and on until she jumped on him, and then he would tickle her, and she would double over with laughter. Billy was a great friend. He filled our home with laughter, and in return we gave him family time that he was missing.

The weather was becoming harsh, so Billy started picking me up in the morning. I was thankful for the warm ride, but mostly I was thankful I wouldn't get a chance to see Jack.

Georgie was discharged just in time; Mary Ann delivered a seven-pound baby boy three days before Christmas. Just like she'd said, having a baby was pretty common. Her mother had had so many that childbirth felt like just a normal event for her. Little John Arthur McDonald came into the world at 3:20 a.m., kicking and screaming. Mary Ann delivered at the hospital, so we didn't get to see John at his first appearance as we had with all of our babies. Georgie said he was chubby, and his hands were big, good for picking junk. They were becoming a beautiful little family. Georgie found them an apartment a couple of blocks away from us, which suited them well. Everyone came to our house for Christmas, including baby John. Billy traveled home to see his mom, and the store was closed for two days after Christmas.

The holiday was a time of much-needed rest and relaxation for me. I cooked and baked to my heart's content. Mary Ann spent most of her time feeding and tending to little John. He had a ferocious appetite and eliminated just as much as he took in. It was such a blessing to hold a little one again. Jackie was captivated by the baby. She never left Mary Ann's side and was quite the little helper. My daughter was growing up so fast, I could scarcely believe it. She had an intense desire to learn. The next school year, she would enter kindergarten, and I believed she was quite ready. I might not have a husband, or Jackie a daddy, but we had family, and it felt good to spend the Christmas holiday with those we loved.

Even Sammy stayed home, leaving behind his business associates, to spend the holiday with us. He called his pool hall friends his "clients." We had little knowledge of what went on in the pool hall but couldn't imagine anything good was going on there. Sammy was a free spirit for sure. He was usually home only to sleep, and some nights he didn't even come home for that; he said he wanted to be ready and available whenever a game came his way. He also had no taste for working a job to get a paycheck. He believed in a get-rich-quick concept of life. Sammy had chosen gaming as his life's work, and none of us could change his mind.

Unlike Sammy, Georgie had gotten a job at a local print shop. He seemed so different since coming home. I guess you could say he was grown up now with a wife and son. I was very proud of him; he was not the same boy whom the school had called a behavior problem.

Billy promoted me to the position of his store assistant at the beginning of January. I was thrilled but also wondered why he'd chosen me. I didn't want our friendship to be the reason I was promoted. I decided to speak to him directly.

"Billy, do you have a minute to chat?"

"Sure, Gracie. I always have time for you."

"I don't mean to be unthankful, and I do appreciate the promotion, but ... did you give me this job because we're friends? If I get a raise or a better job, I would like to think it's because I'm doing a good job."

"Oh, come on, Gracie ... yes, we are friends, but I would never promote you based on that. You are a smart girl, and you've done a fantastic job in your department. It's well organized and efficient, and your scheduling system works better than any department in the store. You have a knack for this business. I could see you having a store of your own someday."

"Thank you, Billy!" I said, a little breathy. "I just didn't want our friendship to be the reason you gave me this job. I wanted to feel that I'd earned it."

He looked down at the floor. "Gracie, I know we're friends, but I hope someday we might be more than that," he said, letting his voice trail off.

I didn't know how to answer him, so I just smiled.

The chamber of commerce sponsored a dinner every year for all the businesses in town. It was especially exciting this year because there were so many new businesses. Billy wanted me to attend the dinner with him because I was his new assistant. The chamber also gave an award every year for the business that had shown the most improvement in sales percentages. Woolworth's had won this year, so Billy would receive an award.

We were so thrilled with the success of the store. He and I had worked hard to get sales up and please our customers. Christmas had been a smashing success. More people had poured into Woolworth's this past year than in the several years past. We'd had pictures with Santa, and elves had given out candy canes and a Christmas coloring book. Once a week, we'd given out free red and green sodas at the lunch counter. We sold Christmas candy hand over fist.

We prided ourselves on keeping our stock up-to-date and

available. If there was anything new on the market, Billy made sure he ordered it and plenty of it. We were a great team. He was easy to get along with, and he didn't pressure me about our relationship. We just worked every day to make the store the best it could possibly be. I began to think that if I never resolved anything with Jack, I might be able to make a life with Billy. He was down to earth and understanding. He loved my family and adored Jackie. What else could I ask for in a husband? I hadn't run into Jack, and I began to think that maybe this was the way it was supposed to be for now. But we were heading into the Easter season, and warm weather was approaching. That meant people would be outside on the street more often.

Billy and I entered the banquet room, and they immediately seated us up front near the platform. We were sitting at a large round table with other associates. The folks who had businesses in town were a competitive bunch but friendly and liked to tease each other. Dinner was served, and it was an all-around enjoyable and amusing evening.

The next event on the agenda was the awards ceremony. The chamber gave many awards, some just for entertainment and others to encourage folks to keep working hard to build their businesses and the city. Billy's award was the most important because he had improved his business almost 40 percent in just one year. He was also awarded for the friendly atmosphere and customer satisfaction that had become well known in our store. I believed that Billy's personality and his genuine ability to make people feel good about themselves had paved the way for our store's success. He deserved all the credit, and I was happy for him.

Finally, the moment came for the award for best sales improvement. The speaker announced Billy Frye, and Billy went to the platform. He received his award and stepped to the mic. "I want to thank the chamber for this wonderful and prestigious award. Since I've moved here, I have found your city to be a welcoming and gracious community. I have met so many people who have gone out of their way to help me and even feed me sometimes. I could not have taken this store into new growth without all the people who have worked together to make this happen. One person I want to introduce who has been instrumental in our success is my assistant manager and dear friend Gracie McDonald. Gracie, please come up."

I was shocked when I heard my name. I had never expected him to call me up in front of all these people. Slowly, I stood up.

"Gracie, don't be shy. You're a big part of this award. Come on up here."

How I made it to the platform, I don't know, because my knees were knocking.

Billy took my hand and drew me to his side. "Folks, this is Gracie. Give her a big hand!"

I looked out over the crowd, feeling very self-conscious. As I scanned the room, my eyes stopped and fixated on a table near the back wall. There sat Jack with his father, next to a beautiful blonde young woman. He looked directly at me, and our eyes locked. I couldn't breathe for an instant, and I felt the color drain from my face. I saw Jack's dad turn his head and look at Jack, but Jack was motionless and continued to look at me. There he was, the only man who could ever fill the void in my heart, staring at me across the room. Finally, I forced a smile at the applauding crowd and turned to leave the platform. Thankfully, Billy had my arm because I was shaking all over. As I sat down, I felt like the lovely dinner we had enjoyed was about to revisit my mouth.

"Gracie, what's wrong with you? Are you sick?"

"No, I just get nervous in front of people."

"Oh, I'm sorry. I didn't mean to put you in a position that was going to upset you."

"It's fine, Billy. I was just surprised and taken a little off guard. I'm fine now," I said as my stomach gave another nauseating churn.

As always, Billy was caring and comforting, always trying

to make me happy. How could I tell him that I had just seen the man I loved and had always loved and probably would love forever? I got through the rest of the evening without vomiting and managed to pull myself together as best as I could. Billy knew something more was going on with me, but he didn't push the issue.

As we were leaving the room, I casually glanced to where Jack had been sitting, and he was gone. I thanked God that he had left. My heart and my mind were flooded with all the old feelings that I had tried so hard to bury. How could I still love this man? After all of the years, all the struggles, how could I want to rush into his arms and never leave? Another thought played around in my mind: Jack had a girlfriend! The beautiful blonde girl sitting by his side must have a connection with him. Why would he bring her to this dinner unless she was important to him? I was glad Billy drove me straight home. I needed to get myself under control and think about all that had transpired. I needed to climb into my bed, my sanctuary, where I was safe. I needed to talk to God and release the tears that had been building for hours. After all the years of trying to forget about Jack, here I was back where I had started, loving him more than words could express. *Dear God, when is this going to end?*

21
Chapter

Our store was busier than ever. I was working six days a week during the Easter rush. I explained to Jackie that this was a busy season, and she smiled and said, "Mommy, I know you are working hard for us. I love you sooo much." She had been adding extra vowels to her words lately, trying to dramatize her thoughts. She was a delight, but it seemed she was growing up so fast that I could barely keep up.

I carried a sack lunch to work now, hiding out in my office to avoid the public when everyone was at the lunch counter. I had no desire to run into Jack and his girlfriend. I knew I was acting a bit childish and not really dealing with my emotions well. I had no idea what to do about Jack or Billy—or anything really.

I could tell Billy was trying to get closer to me. I could see the look in his eyes. Sometimes I would look up and find him staring at me. I knew he was getting serious, and it terrified me. I didn't want to ruin the wonderful relationship we had. I loved working for him, and together we were doing a tremendous job. I could feel myself being squeezed into a corner. Something had to give, and it had to be soon.

After I started eating lunch in the office, he started bringing his lunch to eat with me. I laughed it off at first. "Don't you ever get sick of being in this office?" I said. "I'd think you would want to take a walk and get some air."

"No, I just like to be where you are, Gracie."

His comments were becoming very pointed and direct. I knew it was just a matter of time before he was going to confront me with his feelings. I had no idea what I was going to do. I didn't want to lose my job, and I didn't want to hurt him. Billy was my best friend, and I didn't want to lose his friendship. I could feel the tension between us mounting, so I decided to take a walk after I ate my lunch. I told Billy I had to go to the drugstore and would be back quick.

I headed outside and deliberately turned away from Jack's store. I couldn't chance meeting him now when I had so many other concerns pressing in on me. I was so enjoying the sunshine on my face that I rounded the corner without really paying attention—and ran directly into Jack and his friend. I was too startled to speak for an instant, but I knew I had to say something. "Oh, excuse me. I am so sorry."

"Hello, Gracie. What a surprise."

"Hello, Jack. Yes, this is a surprise."

The blonde woman had a tight grip on his arm. He had been laughing about something until he saw me, and then his face had slowly faded from lighthearted humor to stone-cold animosity. I had never imagined Jack could appear so cold and unfeeling.

"Let me introduce you. This is my fiancée, Linda. Linda, this is an old school friend, Gracie McDonald."

"Oh yes, we saw you at the chamber dinner—your boss won the award. How nice to meet you."

"Yes, it's nice to meet you as well."

"That award was quite an honor. You must be very proud."

"Yes, Billy is really a great manager. I'm very fortunate to work with him. I'm so sorry, but I must run. I'm on an errand for work. Nice meeting you."

Jack looked straight at me with very little expression, and I got away as quickly as possible, before I fell to pieces right in front of them. So Jack was engaged and planning a wedding, and here I was crying myself to sleep every night, praying he would come back to me. What a fool I'd been for believing that what we'd felt as kids would never change. I had been living a life of fantasy, a life built on hopeless dreams that were never meant to come true. I needed to wake up and get into the real world! Jack Wilson had always been out of my league socially— his family had made sure I knew that. Now he wasn't a part of my world at all. He was gone, and I had to learn to live with that. I headed back to work with tears flowing down my face. I had avoided looking at Jack during that chance meeting; I couldn't look into his eyes because he knew me too well. He had always been able to read me when we were together, and I doubted that had changed very much. I had gotten a good look at his Linda. She was very well put together, probably from a well-off family. His parents had always wanted him to marry well, someone in their social circle. It appeared they'd gotten their wish. I dried my eyes and headed back to the office.

Thankfully, Billy was out on the floor somewhere. I had paperwork to do, so I jumped right in and buried myself till it was time to quit for the day. Billy offered to drive me home, but I chose to walk. I told him I needed the exercise. I could pray as I walked, and I needed to pray badly. I was mostly hurt and angry. I didn't know what I had expected from Jack, maybe understanding or compassion. I hadn't expected coldness and indifference. Maybe he was just as surprised as I was and hadn't known what to say either.

After that day, I didn't hide from Jack anymore. I ate at the lunch counter and went outside whenever I wanted. I understood where we stood now. I believed he had forgotten about me and all we had shared. He had moved on to his new life and left the old one in ashes. I had to move on too, form a new way of thinking. I had a newfound passion in me, a new desire to stand up to life as it came and stop wallowing in self-pity. It was time to forge ahead and make a life for Jackie and myself, even if it was not the life I wanted. I heard a scripture in church that said one of God's roles was to "heal the brokenhearted and bind up their wounds." I fit perfectly into that category because my heart was broken, and my wounds were raw. I knew in my mind what I had to do, but my mind and my heart were not in alignment. Some days I felt strong and assertive, and other nights I would cry myself to sleep. It was a tormenting time in my life that left me feeling powerless and confused.

Billy asked me out on a proper date. He said he wanted to talk, and I knew the time had come for him to speak his mind and his heart. He had no idea of what I was dealing with concerning Jack. I had never shared my personal life or any of my feelings with him. I had no idea what I was going to say. I cared about him; he was my best friend. We shared so much together, and our thinking about the store was exactly the same. He was not afraid to let me make decisions and try new promotions. We were having the Easter Bunny booth again and colored chicks. Customers were flocking to the store, and business couldn't have been better. I'd discovered that I had a real gift for management, and Billy had told me many times how impressed he was with my ideas and my enthusiasm. I loved my job, and I loved working with Billy.

My dad was my biggest supporter. He had been with me through every crisis and every heartache. I knew I could depend on him in whatever calamity came my way. But he didn't have much faith when it came to spiritual issues, and he didn't understand the workings of a woman's heart, so I knew I needed to talk to Pastor Kirk. He always straightened me out when my brain and my heart got twisted. I needed to have this talk before I had a date with Billy. I made an appointment and found myself sitting in the same old chair in the pastor's office, sipping a cup of tea.

"I don't know how much of this you want to hear, Pastor. I know you've been married for many years. You and your wife are an inspiration to the whole church."

"Yes, dear, my sweet Ruthie is the love of my life. We have been together since we were kids. She lived on the farm next to me, and we became great friends as children. When I turned eighteen, I asked her father for her hand in marriage. We both knew from the start that we were meant to be together. I guess you could say God ordained it. It seems to me that God designs two people who are meant to spend their lives together. If they find each other, the joy and happiness that result cannot be imagined. We found each other early, and it has been a blessing. Excuse me, dear. You didn't come here to hear about my love life. What is causing you distress?"

"Pastor, I'm having trouble with my love and my life, so what you shared is exactly what I needed to hear." I told Pastor Kirk about Jack and our teenage romance. "Of course, the war intervened in our life just like it did in everyone's. Jackie came along, and you know that whole story. I have never loved anyone like I loved Jack. Even though his family didn't like me when we were teens, they really turned against me after Jackie came along. Over the years we didn't communicate and sort of lost touch. I was ashamed and hid away for months even after Jackie was born."

I continued to pour out my heart about Jack's family, his new fiancée, and all the heartache that I had experienced the last few weeks. I continued to tell him about Billy and the date coming up.

"Pastor, I don't know what to do. I like Billy, but how can I encourage him when I know in my heart that Jack is the love of my life, just like you knew about Ruthie? What do you do when the love of your life doesn't love you back?"

"Ah, lass, you never bring me easy dilemmas, do ye now? Dear, I don't have all the answers, but I do know the one who does. We'll take this to prayer, and I know the great problem solver will work it out. I know one thing for sure: you'll never be happy married to a man who has not captured your heart and soul. True love between a man and a woman is a great mystery that only God Himself understands because He made it so."

I felt much better, as always, after speaking with Pastor Kirk.

I knew he would pray for me. The anger and hurt were beginning to subside, and I had more peace in my heart. I still didn't know what to say to Billy, so I decided to wait and see what he wanted to talk about.

Saturday night rolled around quickly, and Billy and I set out after work for a quiet dinner. We both had been on the go all day. The holiday was approaching, and people were frantic to get everything ready for the big day. Billy had been unusually quiet. Normally, he would joke and cut up with the customers, but not today. He had been all business and focused. I was nervous and a little fearful. I still was not sure what to say or do. We settled in at our table and ordered our meal. I could tell Billy was nervous too; he kept taking sips of water like his mouth was dry. Finally, our meal came, and we ate in silence. I could barely swallow my food, and he looked like he was having the same problem. The dishes were cleared, and there was nothing left to do except talk.

Billy cleared his throat. "Gracie, I want to tell you that you've done a great job since becoming my assistant. I have never had such success with any other store. I have to give you credit for making some really wise suggestions. You're creative and energetic, and I love working with you. We make a really good team, and I want us to continue the good work. I've loved spending time with your family too. Your dad is like a dad to me. Little Jackie is bright and fun, and I love spending time with her. I guess what I'm trying to say is, I want to be more than just your friend and coworker. I want us to have a relationship! I think I'm in love with you and probably have been for a while. Do you think we have a chance to make a life together?"

Here I was, facing this man who meant the world to me. He had given me a chance to become someone I had never thought I could be. I didn't want to hurt him. But I had to admit to myself that I still loved Jack in spite of all the rejection I felt from him. I had to be honest with Billy.

"Billy, you know I care a great deal about you. You are the best friend I have in the whole world. I am eternally grateful for the opportunity you've given me to assist you and to learn. I've never told you about Jackie's father or my life before the war. I want to explain what my life was like, so you understand me. I did not love Jackie's dad. It was a mistake that happened only one time. We were at a party and had been drinking, and I don't even remember how it happened. I separated myself from him and everyone for a long time. I was so full of shame that I didn't want to face people and be looked down on for my mistake. In the midst of that, I found a new faith in God, and He alone has healed me. Jackie's dad died in the war, so I'm her only parent."

"Gracie, I don't condemn you for your life before we met. I assumed there were other men in your life. I knew you had a child. None of that matters to me. I just want to spend my life with you and Jackie. I could be a father to her and a husband to you."

"Billy, there's more. Before Jackie came along, I was in love with someone else, someone I felt was the one person I could spend the rest of my life with. I hate to admit it, but I still have him stuck in my heart. I have tried to wish him away and pray him away, and yet he's still there. I want to be totally honest with you. I can't commit to you or anyone until this obstacle is moved out of my heart. I need time, Billy. I need you to be patient with me."

Billy visibly tensed up and began moving the salt shaker around on the table. He kept his eyes on the table and seemed to be thinking about what to say next. This was a lot to throw at him at one time, and I began to think I should have held some of this back. Billy was my friend, and I trusted him more than anyone I knew, so spilling it all out had seemed perfectly natural to me. Maybe I was right or maybe not. Anyway, it was out there.

Billy looked up with a serious expression. "I can give you time ... if you think there is hope for us someday. Do you think there is, you know, hope?" He lowered his eyes again, hoping for the answer he wanted.

"I promise you that when I'm free of this, you'll be the first to know."

We ended the evening early, and he drove me home. It was a quiet ride because there was much to think about. I didn't have any idea how this would all end, and yet I knew that sometime soon I needed to speak to Jack Wilson alone. There were things I needed to say to him, and I believed there were things he needed to say to me. Maybe after that conversation, we could go on with our individual lives. I had been thinking about how I might contact him for weeks. I had rolled it around in my head with little progress. I knew I needed to get this weight off my shoulders so I could go on and make a life for Jackie and me and maybe Billy too.

22
Chapter

Georgie and his family lived just a few blocks from us. We saw them often, usually at dinnertime. Georgie still had a knack for showing up just as the meal was being put on the table. I had felt a bit of tension between Georgie and Mary Ann when they stopped by to eat or visit recently. I understood how young couples struggled in new marriages, especially when a baby quickly came along before they'd had a chance to get to know each other. In Georgie's case he'd gotten married and left almost immediately for the army. I didn't know all of their personal business. Mama had always said to stay out of other people's business unless they asked you in.

I cared about this young family. Mary Ann was like a sister to me. I knew Georgie was stubborn and had a foul temper at times, but I kept praying they would work everything out between them. One Sunday afternoon, Mary Ann and John Arthur came for a visit. She had never made it to church, even though I kept inviting. She said the baby was too young and would disturb the service. Georgie had refused to go ever since Mama died. I was sure he had some issues with God just like I had.

"Hi, Gracie. Do you think we could talk for a bit?" Mary Ann said as she sat down at the kitchen table.

"Sure. It's nice to see you. How are things?"

Carole Marvin

Tears were beginning to form in Mary Ann's eyes even though she tried to hold them back. "To tell the truth, things are not going well at all," she said as she lowered her eyes. I knew she was trying to hide her tears.

"What's going on? Surely, nothing could be worth all those tears." I rose and took her in my arms, and she collapsed against me. The sobs came fast and hard. I held her until the force of her pain subsided and I thought she could speak coherently. "Mary Ann, what's wrong? I've never seen you like this. Is the baby sick, or Georgie?"

The tears stilled flowed, but she was able to speak. "Gracie, it's Georgie. I can't make him understand that we don't need any more money. His job is taking care of us just fine. I want him home, not out every night trying to get more money. He won't listen to me. I'm really scared for him and us."

"What is he out doing at night to earn money?" I asked, but I already had a sneaking suspicion. I knew my brothers.

Mary Ann continued, "He's been going with Sammy to the pool hall. He said there were ways to make money there, and I didn't need to know any more about it. He's also been coming home smelling like a brewery."

I felt so bad for her. She was thin and tired, and I could see the fear and panic in her eyes. Mary Ann was a good woman, and she didn't need the burden of a man unwilling to communicate his feelings. I had heard this same story from many of my friends since the war ended. It seemed the men had come home closed emotionally, unable to talk about how they felt. So many spent their time at the pool hall or the many beer gardens that had popped up in our community. It appeared that the men needed to talk to other men about their time in the war or just avoid it altogether. It was difficult to share these feelings with their wives and families. Georgie hadn't been in combat, so I didn't understand his need to be drinking with other men.

"Honey, everything is going to be all right. Try to have

some trust in Georgie. You know he loves you and John more than anything. Give it some time, and I'm sure you'll work things out."

Perhaps I shouldn't have been so optimistic, but I didn't know quite what to say, and I didn't want to get in the middle their marriage conflict.

"I don't want Georgie coming home drunk. That really scares me. It's not good for John Arthur to see his daddy like that."

"I agree. Can I do something to help?"

"Gracie, I know Georgie respects you, and he might listen if you talked to him. Would you try to talk some sense into him?"

I hesitated because I knew this was not going to be easy. I saw such fear in her eyes that I reluctantly gave in. "Yes, I will, but I can't promise he'll listen. He's a stubborn boy."

I could have slapped my brother across his head for what he was putting this girl through. I could feel the anger rising in my chest. I would have a talk with him, but first I would have a face-to-face with Sammy, the instigator of it all. I suppose I felt like a mother to my brothers since I had taken that role when Mama died. I didn't get too involved in their lives unless I saw something that rubbed me wrong. Georgie and I had come to blows in the past, and I could take on both my brothers and hold my own. We were stubborn-headed Scots, and we all tried to never give up ground. Sometimes it would get heated when we expressed our opinions, but eventually we'd see eye to eye.

Two nights later, I sat up late, waiting for Sammy to come home. I knew about what time he rolled in after the bars closed. He loved a good time and would stay until the last drink was poured. I needed information about Georgie, and I knew Sammy would give me the lowdown. My brothers were not complicated men, just strong-willed. I knew what it would take to find out what was going on. I heard the door close, and Sammy strolled in with his usual carefree attitude.

"Hey, sis. What are you doing up this time of night?"

"Well, I'm waiting for you, brother."

He eyed me skeptically. "What's on your mind? Ye got that look like you're ready to dig a splinter out of my finger." Sammy made everything into a joke. His whole life had been jokes and games. He never took anything seriously for long and used laughter to weasel out of trouble.

"Sit down, brother. We need to have a chat."

"Well, what's eating at ye?" He plopped down in his chair with a yawn.

"I'll get right to the point: why is Georgie working at Bud's pool room?"

"How should I know why he's there?" he said with a shrug.

"You know very well why he's there. What have you gotten him into?"

"Don't start on me, Gracie. I'm not the one making Georgie work there. You can't blame it on me."

"I'm not blaming you. I just want to know what he's doing there. You're a young, free man, but your brother has a wife and a wee son to think about. Tell me straight out: what is Georgie doing there?" I demanded.

"You know Georgie is a great printer—his letters look like a machine did it. Bud got wind of it, so he asked Georgie to print the race results after the results come in at the track. He's really good at it, and it gives him some extra money for the family."

"So you're saying that all he does is print race results?" I eyed Sammy suspiciously.

"Yea, it gives him extra money, and it's only on Friday and Saturday. It's no big deal, Gracie. Give the man a break."

"Is there betting going on at Bud's?"

"What are you saying? You mean, is he a bookie?"

"Yea, I guess that's what I mean. I'm not sure what that is, but I know it's illegal."

"Nah, nothing like that." He shifted in his chair.

"Then why doesn't Georgie explain it to Mary Ann if he has nothing to hide?"

"How do I know? That's between them. I just go to play pool."

"It sounds to me like there are lots of things going on at Bud's place, and you claim that you don't know any of it?" My brother couldn't fool me.

"I'm going to bed. Let Georgie work out his own problems!" Sammy stomped off.

I had no real understanding of what was going on downtown. I had read in the paper that several new establishments had opened and were run by men of dubious backgrounds. My heart told me that things were not as they appeared. I knew my next conversation would be with Georgie, and I prayed I could handle it carefully and not make him mad. Georgie could be a handful when he got his dander up.

It was a week before I could get Georgie to stop by for a chat. He walked in the back door already defensive. "So you're calling me on the carpet, are ye? I know Mary Ann talked to you. I'm just trying to support my family. My wage from the print shop isn't enough to keep us going."

"I understand that, but do you have to be gone every night? She needs you home with her and the baby."

"I'm not gone every night! It's only two nights a week. You know, Gracie, I did a very foolish thing when I quit school at twelve years old. I haven't got any skills to get a good job. Picking junk and working at the print shop pays very little."

"Have you explained that to your wife? Do you ever talk to her?"

"Yes, of course I do, but she doesn't understand. I need to support my family, and Bud is giving me a chance to do that."

"Mary Ann said you've been coming home smelling like a brewery. We all went through that with Dad. Why would you do that to your family?"

"Gracie, enough said. It's my business what I drink and how I make my living. Remember what mum used to say: stay out of it."

Carole Marvin

That was the end of our conversation. Georgie was up and out the back door before I could say another word. The talking was done; now it was time to pray.

Billy spent Easter with us, and he brought Jackie two baby chicks. She squealed with delight and quickly named them Joe and Mo even though they were hens. Dad built a small cage in the backyard to keep the cat away from them. Time was moving quickly, and I had yet to have my meeting with Jack. Billy had been extremely patient with me. We were just enjoying each other's company. Our conversations were not deep, although at times I felt he wanted to ask how I was feeling about things, especially about him. He restrained himself well and didn't push me, and I was thankful.

I formed a plan in my mind and prayed it would work. This hole in my heart needed to mend. I was so tired of longing for Jack and everything we could have had. I knew God had forgiven me for my transgressions and loved me. My biggest problem was the regret. I regretted that I had lost the love of my life, the man who had been created just for me, and I feared no one else could ever take his place.

A few days later I told Billy that I needed a two-hour lunch because I had errands that couldn't wait. He was always agreeable and supportive of me. I decided to be straightforward and march right into Jack's store and look him in the eye. I wasn't going to beat around the bush anymore. I had always been a bit assertive but had lost some of it over the years. It seemed that after Jackie was born, my high-spirited attitude had been crushed. I thought now before I spoke and weighed my words. Dad said I was wiser now, but I thought it was shame. I was living the life of a woman with a child and no husband. This was not thought of as acceptable, and I was aware of it. At the same time, I was not going to let the fact that I was a woman stop me from being strong and independent. I mustered up as much courage as I could and crossed the street to Jack's store. I had never gone near this business for fear of running into Jack or his dad. I opened the door and marched right in, feeling a surge of adrenaline.

The store was beautiful. Every part was set up like a room from someone's home. There were living rooms and bedrooms, completely furnished and decorated. I was very impressed and somewhat intimidated. I knew Jack's family lived well and traveled in social circles that were well above the reach of the average person. I understood his family, and I also understood he loathed that way of life. He had always said they were arrogant, and he never wanted to be like them. The store was his family come to life because it reeked of haughtiness and everything that was distasteful to him. I felt a sense of sadness wash over me. He had become what he had once despised, and it broke my heart.

I walked around, looking at the fine furniture and admiring all of the modern impressive styles. This space was truly a work of art. I sensed someone behind me and turned to face Linda, Jack's fiancée.

"May I help you?" she asked sweetly.

She was very polished and sophisticated. I did a sweeping glance of her clothes and could tell she came from means. Mildred must have picked this girl out special for Jack. There was no doubt she was perfect.

"Thank you. I'm just browsing. You have a lovely store." I lowered my eyes.

"Yes, we are very pleased with how it has turned out. We have all the best brands, and Mr. Wilson still makes many of the pieces himself. We take special orders for handmade pieces, you know, if you're looking for anything special. Mr. Wilson is such a craftsman."

She didn't seem to recognize me, so I just continued the conversation.

"Yes, I can see the workmanship is quite impressive. Who is the manager of this store?"

"Oh, that would be my fiancé, Jack Wilson." She still didn't seem to recognize me, and I was thankful for that.

"I see. Would he be available to speak with me?"

"Yes, I suppose so, but I'm sure I could help with whatever you need."

"No, I'm afraid not. It's a … specific matter. I need to speak with him personally and privately." My heart was racing.

Linda appeared to be taken aback when I said "privately." Nevertheless, she pulled herself together and had begun to walk away when she suddenly turned and said, "Aren't you Jack's friend from high school?"

My stomach lurched. "Uh, yes, I am. We met a few weeks ago outside."

"Oh yes, now I remember." She smiled and quickly scampered off to find Jack.

I didn't want to be harsh with her; it wasn't her fault that she'd fallen in love with someone whom I also loved. She had no way of knowing or even understanding what my life with Jack had been before she came along. I needed to show compassion and self-control. I waited a few minutes, and then there he was, walking toward me with a serious, tense look in his eye. Linda wasn't following him; she apparently took the word "private" seriously.

"Hello, Jack." I took a deep breath. "How are you?"

He didn't answer right away. I saw the tension in his face and could tell he was most uncomfortable.

"I am sorry to bother you at work, but I needed to talk to you. I have been thinking about having a conversation for a long time but couldn't bring myself to do it until now." My palms were beginning to sweat, and my throat was dry. I had so much to say but couldn't get the words out of my mouth.

Before I could continue, Jack jumped in, impatient to get this over with. "Gracie, we have nothing to talk about. Our lives have taken different directions, and we need to leave it that way."

The coldness in his voice was a shock to my system. This

was a man I didn't even know. "I understand how you feel," I said, "but I need to have one conversation with you so I can move on with my life. Believe me, I'm happy that you are moving forward, and I would hope you would give me the opportunity to do the same." My eyes pleaded with him. *Please, Jack, give me this one chance.*

"Gracie, I really don't want to talk to you!" Jack hissed. "You caused me so much heartache, and it's taken me a long time to recover, and I don't want to think about it ever again." He wouldn't look at me directly. He focused behind me or at the floor, but he never looked into my eyes. We had always been able to read each other if we made eye contact, so he shut out that communication too. Jack put his hands in his pockets and sighed deeply. It was obvious he wanted this conversation to end as quickly as possible.

"Please, Jack, I suffered too … in ways you'll never understand. I know I might not deserve it, but all I ask is that you give me the chance to explain so I can move on in my life."

He sighed again. "What do you want from me, Gracie?"

"I want you to meet me and let me tell you everything that happened to me and us. That's all."

I could see the pain in his eyes. I had been through heartache and hurt, but I saw something in him that made me question the comparison I was making. I began to realize that his pain was far greater than mine. He had been in the war and had been shot. He had seen unimaginable things in combat. He was suffering from the same issues as most of our soldiers, and yet he continued to move forward in his life. I suddenly felt selfish and ashamed of myself.

"I'm sorry, Jack. Maybe this was bad idea. I'll respect your wishes and stay away from you. I just ask that you please forgive me for all the hurt I caused. I have so many regrets that at times I feel as if I'll choke on them. If I could go back, I would do things differently, and maybe we would have found happiness together. I won't bother you again." Hot tears sprang to my eyes.

I took one final look into his face and saw tears forming in his eyes too. Afraid I couldn't hold myself together, I quickly turned and walked out of the store. There was a small plaza in the middle of town with trees and benches. I found a bench that was somewhat private and sat down because my knees were shaking. I felt as if my heart had just been split in two. I realized that it was over—Jack was gone, and he never wanted to see me again. All the hope that I had carried deep in my heart was gone too. I had lost him. He belonged to someone else now. I let the tears come; I was incapable of holding them back. I had carried a false hope that someday Jack would want me back, and everything would be like it had been. That idea had shattered in minutes, and my world with it. "God, please help me!" I said out loud as sobs shook my body.

I don't know how long I sat there shaking and sobbing. People walked by, glancing at me. I needed to go home. I could call Billy later and make some excuse. I needed to get out of the city, and I needed to do it quickly. Walking home helped relieve the tension in my body, but my heart was still in pieces.

I managed to get through the evening. I put Jackie to bed and held her tight.

"Mommy, you're squeezing me too tight!"

"Sorry, sweetheart. I just love you so much I can't stop."

"Mommy, can we go to the park this Sunday after church? I want to go on that big kid's swing again. I can hold on really tight now, and you can push me real high. Maybe Robert and his Mommy would like to go. We could have a picnic and stay the whole afternoon!"

"That sounds like a great idea, honey. Let's plan on it."

Jackie settled down, and I turned in early. I needed the safety of my bed, where I could talk to God and cry myself to sleep once again. What was I going to do now? I knew that God had a plan for me. Pastor Kirk had told me that many times. What that plan involved was a mystery. I cried myself to sleep, and this was just the beginning of many tearful nights.

23

Chapter

When you have a five-year-old living in your house, life goes on without delay. Jackie was up early Sunday morning, excited about church and her trip to the park. She was an active little girl, and her enthusiasm was not unlike my own at her age. We invited Annie and little Robert to go with us. They had been coming to church regularly, and occasionally Robbie would come with them. He had been doing well. He was getting counseling from the government through the GI Bill. He was also enrolled in a training program to become a plumber.

Annie was another sister to me. She was Bo's sister and Jackie's aunt. She would always be family. I didn't think of Bo often. He had been part of a tragic and devastating period in my life. Dwelling on it only brought me sadness and pain. That night five years earlier had altered the course of my life, and I had questioned God about it many times. He had shown me one day that all the things that had happened to me were what had driven me to Him. After that revelation, I never considered questioning Him again.

My life was in God's hands, and I needed to trust Him. I had been holding on to an idea of how I wanted my life to be, and now I had to let go and let God paint the picture. I would always love Jack, but I needed to put that aside and find a life with someone else. I needed someone who would love me and

Carole Marvin

Jackie. She needed a father, and I needed a husband, someone who would take care of us. Every child needs a home and the love of two parents. I could learn to love someone who offered me security and companionship. Love didn't have to be fireworks and atomic blasts. It could be quiet contentment and mutual respect. Two people could find peace with each other and work together to build a life. Jack had found his new life, and now I needed to find mine.

Sunday was a perfect day. The sun was bright, and the air was warm. Jackie was beside herself with excitement. It really didn't take much to make her happy. Even though she had a rather abnormal childhood with a working mom and no father, she was a happy little girl. She was smart and cooperative and saw the good in everyone. I never thought for a moment that her life was deficient in any way, but she needed a father to balance her thinking about men. My own my father had helped shape my image of myself. He had helped me form opinions about life and had given me confidence to step out and take on the world. He had taught me to love my country and fight for a piece of the American dream. He'd taught me to work hard and never give up. My mother had been my heart, but my dad was my soul. I didn't want Jackie to miss out on that kind of relationship. I wanted her to respect men and someday find someone who would love her like my dad loved my mum.

After church we headed to the park with our lunch. We always spread our blanket on a grassy area near the playground. The kids quickly gulped down their sandwiches and chips. "Mommy, I'm going to play on the carousel with Robert, and then you can push me on the big swing, okay?" Jackie sure liked to be in charge of the plan! I allowed her the freedom in small issues, but I corrected her bossiness in big ones. I guess you could say I chose my battles.

"All right, sweetheart. You come get me when you're ready to swing."

Off the children went, hand in hand. They were great

friends, and I was thankful that Jackie had a cousin. Annie and her family were my family too. I confided most of my heartaches and frustrations in her.

"How is work going?" Annie asked.

"Fairly well. I love my job. It seems I'm pretty good at store management. Who would have thought it?"

"You managed your parents' home for years. Why would you not be good?"

"I guess I never thought of myself as a boss."

"Gracie, you can be the bossiest person I know."

I laughed at that because I knew she was right. "Billy doesn't seem to mind me making decisions. All the promotions we've done have been my idea. Most of them have been successful."

"I thought the bunny booth was great. There were kids lined up every time I was in the store."

"Christmas and Easter have been our most successful seasons since the store's been in operation. Billy is really pleased with how things are going."

"Is he pleased with how *you and he* are doing?" she asked with a mischievous smile.

"He tries not to talk about us, but I know he probably is running out of patience with me."

"Well, what are you going to do?"

"I went to see Jack at his store a couple of days ago. Did I forget to mention that?" I said sheepishly.

"Oh my goodness, Gracie, what happened?"

"I tried to arrange a meeting with him just to talk. I wanted to apologize and clear the air. He was cold and nervous. He said we had nothing to talk about, and he wanted me to leave him alone. He looked tired and worried. He made it very plain that he wants nothing to do with me. He said I caused him enough pain, and he didn't want to talk about any of it."

"Oh, Gracie, I am so sorry. You must be feeling terrible."

"I've cried myself to sleep every night. There is nothing more I can do. I have to get over this and make some decisions about Billy. I just can't seem to get rid of this huge rock in my chest where my heart is supposed to be."

"Gracie, give yourself some time. Healing will come."

"I know, Annie, but how long will it take? I feel like my life is on hold in the relationship department."

Jackie came running across the playground and jumped into my arms. "I'm ready to swing, Mommy!"

"Okay, honey, let's see how high we can go."

My little girl was growing up. She held on tight as I pushed her higher and higher. I was trying to teach her to pump her legs, so she could swing herself, when I saw her slide sideways. I grabbed the swing and slowed it down just in time. She was starting to cry, so I grabbed her to me.

"It's okay, baby. I got you. I guess Mommy pushed you a little too high." As I held her close, brushing the hair from her eyes, I felt the presence of someone behind me.

"Is your little girl okay?"

I turned and looked up right into the face of Jack's girlfriend, Linda. She looked as startled as I was.

"Oh yes, she's fine. We just went a little too high. She's just learning to do the big swings."

"Jack, come here! It's your old high school friend! Her little girl almost slid off the swing."

My heart was in my throat as I saw Jack walking toward us. I didn't know what to do.

Jackie had stopped crying and now was squinting up at Linda and Jack. "Who is this lady, Mommy?"

"Hello, I'm Linda. What is your name?"

"My name is Jackie Armstrong," Jackie said politely.

"Well, Jackie, it's very nice to meet you. This is Jack, my fiancé. Isn't it funny you both have kind of the same name?" she said with a smile.

Jack looked directly into my eyes. The look of shock on his face was apparent to me but I hoped not to Linda.

Jackie had never been shy, so I was not surprised when she looked at Linda and asked, "What does fiancé mean?"

"It means that my Jack and I are getting married."

"When are you doing that?"

"We are planning it for early September, about two months from now."

"Can I come to your wedding?"

I grabbed Jackie by the arm and tilted her head up to make eye contact. "Sweetheart, you don't invite yourself to someone's wedding. That is considered rude."

"Honey, I would love for your mommy to bring you to the wedding. She is, after all, an old high school friend of my Jack. Isn't that right, Jack?"

"Can we, Mommy?"

Jack stood staring at all three of us, not knowing what to say or do. He was so different from how he used to be. I remembered him always laughing, making jokes, always knowing what to say to lighten the mood. The man standing in front of me was quiet, tense, and full of anxiety. I could see the rigid line of his jaw tightening the longer he stared at us. This was not the Jack I knew and loved.

"Jackie, sweetheart, we need to go. Thank you for humoring Jackie, Linda. She has never been to a wedding, so she doesn't quite understand. I wish you both all the happiness in the world."

Linda smiled and took Jack's hand. "Thank you. We are very happy."

Jack didn't look happy. In fact, he looked as if he needed to vomit.

"Nice seeing you both," I said. I took Jackie's hand, and we moved quickly back to Annie and the safety of our picnic area. My heart was pounding like a drum. I never could have imagined this afternoon turning out so badly. *God, help me to let this go!*

"Gracie, what's wrong? You look like you've seen a ghost."

"I just ran into Jack and his future wife. He looked so tense and angry."

"Maybe the war has affected him just like everyone else. Maybe he's fighting the same demons that Robbie is fighting. I understand it a little, but no one completely understands what it was like or what these men went through. Pray for him, Gracie. It's a horrible way to live."

I felt deflated. "Jack is getting married in two months. How am I ever going to live through that?"

24

Chapter

Pastor Kirk had been teaching about a word that was somewhat foreign to me: surrender. It seemed that when we couldn't fix a problem in our lives, we needed to surrender it to God and let Him fix it. I came from a long line of stubborn Scots, and we typically didn't surrender to anything or anybody, and we didn't give up on someone who belonged to us. Jack was mine; he had been mine since we were kids. I prayed every night that God would call off the wedding or help me accept it and have peace. I considered the pastor's words and decided to try to let it go and let God handle it. I wasn't having much success doing it my way, so why not let the Almighty do it?

I had to make some decisions about Billy. He was breathing down my neck, wanting a decision about our relationship. I had been trying to avoid him as much as possible lately.

He walked into the office one Saturday afternoon, ready to talk. "Gracie, how are you doing? Haven't seen you all day."

"I've been in here working. I got all the inventory finished."

"I was wondering if your dad would sit with Jackie tonight and if we could spend an evening together. I haven't seen you much lately."

"Oh, I don't know, Billy. I'm awfully tired."

"Gracie, give me a break. I think you're trying to stay away from me. I understand your feelings concerning Jack, but didn't he tell you he didn't want to see you again?"

"Yes, he did tell me that."

"Then why are you holding on to someone who doesn't want you?"

"I don't know."

"Yet you're willing to let me drag along, hoping for something that might never be."

"Billy, please understand. I care very much for you. You're my best friend. I've told you everything about me, and you've never judged me. I appreciate the job you've given me and all you've taught me."

"Yes, you like me, and you appreciate me. You just don't love me. Let's be really honest—do you ever see a future with me?"

I was struck dumb. How could I tell him that I could never love anyone but Jack? Here I was again, hurting someone who truly cared about me. It seemed all I did was turn men away who really loved me and then end up alone. "Billy, please give me some more time."

"Sure, take all the time you need. Why not?" He turned and stomped out of the office, slamming the door behind him.

I felt the tears start sliding down my face. He was right: I didn't love him. I cared about him, but not enough to build a life with him. I had put myself in a prison, and only God could break me free. The word *surrender* kept flashing through my mind like a neon sign: *All things are possible to those who believe if you surrender.* I dried my eyes and began to close things down for the weekend. I knew what I needed to do, but how could I when every beat of my heart brought Jack's face to my mind? My mind said I need to surrender it all to the Lord, but my heart shouted loud and clear that I would never let him go. "I promise you, Lord, I will try to surrender it to you."

Jackie was ready to head to the park after church on Sunday. She was making a habit of asking to spend Sunday afternoon with me and the big-girl swings. I didn't mind; I loved being out in the sun. Annie and Robert couldn't go this time, so we struck out on our own. The trees were in full bloom, and the sun was unusually bright, with not a cloud in the sky. There was a soft breeze, and I spread my blanket on our favorite grassy spot. Jackie ate her lunch quickly as usual and went off to the playground. I had time now to think and pray. I lay back on the blanket and closed my eyes to drink in the sun's rays. It felt so warm and calming that I nearly fell asleep. I knew Jackie was all right; she had found a couple of little girls to play with in the sandbox. I thought I was dreaming when I felt a shadow block the sun's rays. I opened my eyes and sat up and looked straight into the eyes of Jack staring down at me.

"Jack, what are you doing here?" I could hardly believe my eyes.

"Hello, Gracie."

I had no idea what to say to him. He looked tired and lost. The deep hurt that I had noticed in his eyes the last time I saw him was still there.

"May I sit down?" he asked.

"Yes, of course." I moved over to make room for him.

"I came here today on purpose. I hoped you would be here."

"My daughter loves the park." I still had no idea what to say.

"Is that her over there in the sandbox?"

"Yes, she found a friend."

"Remember when you came into the store and wanted to talk?"

"Yes, you said you never wanted to talk to me again. I remember it quite well." I looked down at my hands, saddened by the memory.

"I'm sorry I was so harsh. You surprised me, and I wasn't prepared to talk to you. I believe now that you were right; we do need to clear the air, especially since I'm getting married in a couple of months."

I felt that familiar sting again—he was almost a married

man. "Yes, you don't need to take anger and unforgiveness into a new marriage."

"What do you mean, 'unforgiveness'?" he asked.

"It seems you're still carrying anger toward me, even though I wrote to you and explained everything and asked for forgiveness," I said.

"I never got a letter from you. I was gone for years in the heat of the battle, and I never heard from you, not once."

"I only wrote you one letter because I was too ashamed to tell anyone about what was happening in my life. I did write two years ago and told you everything about me."

"I never got it, Gracie."

I just looked at him. I didn't know what to say next. "What do you want to know, Jack?"

"Who's your little girl's father?"

It pained me to hear this question, but I promised to surrender all of this to God and let Him handle it.

"She's Bo's little girl. We were at a party, and I drank too much, and he took advantage of me. I don't even remember it happening. I was so shocked and humiliated that I refused to ever speak to him again. It was awful when it happened, but discovering I was pregnant made it even worse. I have lived with the guilt and condemnation every day since."

"Where is Bo now"?

"He was killed two years ago. I have no one special in my life, just Jackie and me. I've raised her on my own with Dad's support."

"Well, I guess you have been fighting your own little war. I'm sorry that Bo took advantage of you." His look was genuine.

"You could say I've been in a war. It's not easy being a mom with no husband."

Jackie came running over, covered in sand. "Mama, I'm thirsty. Can I have a drink?"

"Sure, honey. Brush the sand off first."

"Who is this man, Mommy?"

"This is my friend Jack. We met him last week at the park with his fiancée, remember?"

"Yeah, she was pretty. They're getting married, right, Mommy?"

"Yes, honey, you're right."

"Why does he have the same name as me?"

Jack looked at me, asking the same question with his eyes. He still had those beautiful blue eyes that had always melted my heart.

"Well, I guess there are lots of people with the same names …" I trailed off, not knowing what to say.

Luckily, kids didn't always require a full explanation. Jackie quenched her thirst and was off again to the sandbox.

"Why did you name her Jackie?"

"Her full name is Emma Jacqueline McDonald. She's named after my mother and you because you were the two people I loved most in the world."

He looked at me the way he used to look at me, not just into my eyes but into my heart. I had to turn my eyes away because I couldn't let him see the pain and heartache that I carried with me every day of my life.

"I guess I'd better go," he said. "I'm glad we could do this. I hope this helps you move on with your life, Gracie."

"Thank you, Jack, for talking to me. I really appreciate it. I'm learning in church that forgiveness is the key to everything. I hope you will forgive me for how I hurt you."

"I guess I'll have to think about that." He got up and left as quickly as he had appeared.

It took me the rest of the afternoon to calm myself and get my mind focused back on God.

25

Chapter

I got into the office early on Monday so I could bury myself in work before Billy found me. I knew I wasn't being fair to him, but I had nothing to offer him right now, and I didn't want to give him false hope.

He found me just after the store opened, and I could see the hurt in his eyes. "Gracie, I'm sorry for storming out of here on Saturday. I just wanted to know where I stood with you, and now I guess I know. I won't pressure you anymore."

"Billy, I'm sorry too. I—"

"Say no more. We'll just be friends."

"I would love to continue being your friend. You mean the world to me."

He went to his desk and left me with my thoughts. I had such admiration for this man, and I wanted to keep the friendship, yet I knew things could never be the same between us again.

Mary Ann met me for lunch. I hadn't seen her in a while, and she looked tired and worried. John Arthur was sitting in his stroller, chewing on a teething biscuit. He was growing so quickly. I wondered if his daddy was spending any time with him. Georgie hadn't come around to the house since our last squabble. He certainly didn't want me telling him what to do.

"How have you been, Mary Ann?"

"I'm okay. Just trying to keep my mind on John and off of Georgie." She looked annoyed.

"Why would you not want to think about your husband?"

"He doesn't act like a husband. He's out most every night and comes home with alcohol on his breath. I can't talk to him without him getting angry. I don't know what kind of a marriage I got myself into, but it's not what I expected." I could tell that Mary Ann's heart had hardened a little bit since we last spoke. A woman could put up with only so much.

"I am so sorry, honey. I wish there was something I could do." That brother of mine! If he only knew what he had.

"No one can do anything. I'm just stuck and miserable."

We continued our lunch together and chatted a bit, but neither of us brought up the subject of my brother again. I cared deeply about my family, and I wanted the best for them, so I decided to begin praying for my brother and Mary Ann daily. It seemed God was the only answer for any of us.

Aunt Martha was preparing for a visit. We hadn't seen Jane for months. She had gone to kindergarten and would enter first grade in the fall. Jackie loved having her visit, and I felt close to Mama whenever she was near. She was a beautiful little girl, and of course, she looked just like Mama. Aunt Martha and her family were doing a wonderful job raising her. They were a wholesome, loving family. Their home was full of laughter and peace. Our home had been like that until death stole my brother and my mama. I had fun with Jackie, but the general climate of our home was still sadness, even after all these years. I hadn't visited my aunt and her family in many years, so I promised myself that I would make a visit very soon. Jackie needed to see how a real happy family lived. That was the kind of home I wanted for her and me.

"Jane, sweetheart, how you've grown! Ready to start first grade, are ye?"

"Yes, I'm six years old now. I love school. I'm going to be a teacher someday!"

"That's wonderful, honey. I know you'll be a fine teacher."

"Come here, lass," called Dad. "Come see your daddy. I've missed you, sweet girl." Dad always had tears in his eyes when he saw Jane. He loved her and cherished the times they had together.

We all loved Jane, but Jackie couldn't get enough of her. She had trouble understanding how Jane was her aunt, but that never stopped her from devouring as much of her attention as possible. Once these two girls got together, the rest of us were pushed to the side. They went upstairs to play school, which gave the adults a chance to talk, and the focus was turned on me.

"Gracie, do you like your job?" Aunt Martha asked.

"Yes, I love my job. I'm assistant manager of the whole store now. I have a great boss. He's taught me everything about the business."

"Yea, we all love Billy," said my dad. "I don't understand why Gracie doesn't marry him. He's clearly smitten with her!" Dad gave me a wink.

"Dad, stop. Billy and I are just friends."

"Well, I'm sure he sees things a little differently. You better find someone soon, girl. You're not getting any younger."

"Gracie, you need to wait for the right guy," Aunt Martha said. Don't settle for just anyone. Once you're married, it's for life. You want to make sure you really find the right one."

I did find the right one, I thought, *only to lose him to someone else.*

We spent most of the afternoon talking about the good old days when Aunt Martha and mama were girls. She remembered a time when Mama fell out of a tree and broke her arm. The doctor set it, but the pain was excruciating. Aunt Martha sat up all night, praying and singing with Mama. They were both sisters and friends.

"Aunt Martha, the Lord has been teaching me about

surrender. It means when you can't fix a problem, you just give it up and let Him fix it. He knows best anyway."

"Yes, we all need to learn to give things to God, and the challenge is to never take them back."

Whenever we got to talking about God, Dad always went out to the backyard for a breath of fresh air. He didn't have much use for talking about God. I believed he still blamed Him for taking Mama.

"Aunt Martha, can I ask you something?"

"Sure, honey, anything."

"Five years ago, when I was in high school, I had a boyfriend named Jack Wilson. Do you remember Mama speaking of him?"

"Yes, I do remember Emma speaking of him. She said you two were so in love."

"That was true, and he wanted to get married right after high school. I wasn't ready to settle down, so I broke it off. He went to the war, and I had Jackie. He was hurt and angry with me, and I never saw him again for years. He's back from the war now and engaged to someone else. Aunt Martha, I still love him, and I don't think I can ever love anyone else."

"My dear, you are in a pickle." She looked at me with concern and compassion. "I do see why you're taking an interest in surrender. What are you going to do? It's not easy loving someone who doesn't seem to love you back!"

"I guess I have to surrender it to God. What else can I do?"

"Have you spoken to him about how you feel?"

"I've had a couple of conversations with him, and I think he has forgiven me for my foolishness, but he's engaged to be married in one month. What can I possibly do about that?"

"You can at least tell him how you feel. He deserves to know the truth about your feelings. Then he can make up his own mind. You do all you can do, and then God will do the rest. Surrender is not giving up; it's doing what you can do and letting God do what you can't do."

"I guess I never realized that I had a part to play in all this."

"Honey, God always works with us. He never excludes us from the process. He's your heavenly father, and He's concerned about everything that concerns you."

Aunt Martha made a lot of sense. Before now, I'd never felt that I should intervene in Jack's relationship with Linda. I had felt that he had a new life, and I should stay out of his way. I went to bed that night with a newfound purpose. I needed to tell Jack how I was feeling and then let him decide what he wanted to do with his marriage and his life. I couldn't make him want me over Linda, but I could at least tell him the whole truth. I owed that to him and to myself.

At work the next day, I decided to take a break and headed to the lunch counter. I had a craving for a chocolate soda, and our soda jerks made the best in town. We were busy, and the stools were all full except for one. I plopped myself down and glanced at the person next to me. I then turned my head in the other direction and came face-to-face with Jack.

"Jack, um, hi," I said cautiously.

He looked startled and uneasy, as he always seemed to be around me. "Gracie, hi. Are you having lunch?"

"I got a hankering for a soda, and we make the best."

"I like your lunch counter. Your store has a lot to offer."

"Yeah, Billy is a really good manager and a great guy."

"Is he your boyfriend then?"

That question shocked me a little. I didn't think he'd noticed that Billy and I spent time together. "We dated some. I appreciate the opportunities he's given me. He has taught me so much about running a business, and I'm grateful to him."

"Sounds like you care about him."

"I do care about him, but he's not my boyfriend."

Jack just looked at me, and those piercing eyes melted my heart.

"I guess you'll be a married man soon."

"Yeah, the wedding is a month away."

"Well, I hope you'll be very happy," I mustered the courage to say.

"Honestly, Gracie ... I don't think I'll ever be really happy."

My heart felt as if it were about to explode in my chest. He looked at me again with those eyes that seemed to penetrate my soul. I met his gaze, and I could feel my eyes filling up with tears.

"I understand what you mean. Sometimes I don't think I'll ever be happy either."

The air between us was so thick with tension that I could hardly breathe.

He stopped eating and pushed his food away. "Gracie, I've been thinking about what you said to me in the park about forgiveness. I think I have forgiven you. I understand that you were young and not ready to settle down. I don't fault you for that. I was impatient and wanted you so much ... I guess we were both immature. The war forced me to look at life full in the face and accept things the way they were, even if I didn't like it. I had to grow up quick. I saw things that one should never have to see. It left a wound in my soul that may never heal."

"I'm so sorry, Jack. The war affected us all in some way. I think we all grew up quick. I hope my foolishness didn't contribute to your unhappiness."

"Gracie, I don't really know where you fit in my memory. I remember what it was like with us, and I think about how I felt then and how I feel now. I can't really put into words what I feel, but just know I've let all the past hurt go. You owe me nothing."

It's now or never, I thought. *Come on, Gracie, be brave!* I climbed off my stool and looked Jack square in the face. "I have only one thing to say to you, Jack: I still love you, and you'll always be in my heart. We belong together, and I don't think either of us will be happy with anyone else."

I had really opened up, and everything had just spewed out. He looked stunned and shocked, but at least I had done my part, and now it was up to God. I turned and walked away as quickly as possible. I couldn't look back at him. My heart was pounding like a bass drum, and my palms were sweating. I closed the door to my office and tried to calm down. I knew I had shocked Jack; I had even shocked myself! It all had shot out like a bullet from a gun.

I can't explain what happened next except to say it was a miracle. I sat down in my chair, and a warm sense of calm washed over me. It was as if I was wrapped in a warm blanket, safe and secure. I had never felt such peace. It was unexplainable and wonderful at the same time. *Surrender. Surrender.* I had been thinking about surrender for weeks. I had tried every which way to figure it out, and in a simple moment I had experienced it. It was like I had been living under a cloud, and now that cloud was gone, and the sun's rays were shining directly on me. It was all in God's hands now. Whatever happened from now on was the path God had chosen for me, and I had accepted it and was thankful. I knew now that I would be all right.

26

Chapter

I decided to plan a trip to visit Aunt Martha and her family. She lived about fifty miles away in Woodburn, Indiana. It was a small town surrounded by farms. The people were simple, God-fearing folks. Jim, Martha's husband, owned a small hardware store. It had been his dad's store, and he'd inherited it when his dad died. Martha worked as a teacher's helper at Woodburn Elementary School. They had two teenage boys, Jeff and Eli, who kept their lives interesting. The family attended the community church, and to me they were a perfect family. Their home was full of love and fun.

We used to visit them every summer when Mama was alive. There were always picnics and swimming in the creek and a million other things for kids to do. Uncle Jim had taught my brothers and me how to bait a hook and then unhook it from the fish's mouth. I loved those times we spent in the country. We had always lived in the city and had a brick sidewalk instead of grassy fields. I needed to feel the warmth of this home, and I wanted Jackie to experience what a real family was like.

"Billy, I need a vacation. Do you suppose I could have a few days off? I want to take Jackie to visit my aunt in Woodburn. I know Saturdays are busy, but things are slow right now."

Billy talked to me only when it concerned business now. There was no personal communication between us. I knew I had hurt him, but I couldn't do anything about it. I had been honest with him, and he needed to accept things as they were.

"Yes, you can have some time off, and when you get back, I'm taking a few days myself. I want to visit my mother."

"Is your mother well?"

"She's having a few problems, and I need to check on her. Taking time now before the back-to-school rush is a good idea; we'll really start getting busy in August."

"I'm sorry to hear about your mum."

"None of your concern," he said dryly.

That was the end of our conversation. That was the way things were with us now, short and to the point. I understood, but I missed the old Billy who had always made me laugh. I prayed he would find someone who would love him the way he deserved, but that someone wasn't me.

I had everything ready to go. We were taking the bus, and it was Jackie's first time. She was beyond excited. Her eyes were as big as saucers when we took our seats.

"Mama, how long will it take us to get to Aunt Martha's house?"

"Around two hours or so. You need to sit back and enjoy the ride."

"Mama, does Jane have a dog? I've always wanted a dog."

"I don't know. Maybe."

"How old are my boy cousins?"

"Their names are Jeff and Eli, and they are fourteen and sixteen. You need to call them by their names."

"Do they go fishing with their daddy?"

"I don't know, honey."

"Does Aunt Jane have her own room?"

"I'm pretty sure she does. I don't think the boys want her in their room."

"Are we almost there?"

"Jackie, get out your coloring book and color a little. It will make the time go faster."

We arrived in less time than anticipated, and by then I was tired out from all the questions. Aunt Martha and Jane met the bus and walked us to their house. It was a beautiful day, and I felt so free from everything I'd left behind. For me, the struggle was over; it was in God's hands now.

"Jackie, we're going to have so much fun!" exclaimed Jane. "I can't wait to show you my room. I set it up just like a schoolroom. I'm going to be the teacher, and you'll be a kindergarten kid like I was last year. I'll teach you all your letters and numbers. Do you know your colors yet?"

"Gracie, I'm afraid Jane has the whole week planned. I hope Jackie can keep up with her," Aunt Martha laughed.

I smiled. "Believe me, they are cut from the same cloth. It will be interesting to see who gives out first."

"Gracie, it's so nice having you here. Remember all the summers you spent here with your mama?"

"Yes, your home was like a little piece of heaven for me. Where are your boys?"

"Jim makes them work at the store. He says every kid needs to learn to work."

"He's not wrong about that; you don't want them to turn out like Sammy."

"Is he still hanging out at the pool hall?"

I rolled my eyes. "Yes, he says playing pool is his job. I don't understand him, Martha. He was raised like the rest of us."

"Losing your dear mama affected your whole family. They all have reacted in different ways."

"Georgie and Mary Ann are struggling too. He's under pressure about money, so he works all the time, and he's drinking lots of beer."

"Honey, when they get married and leave home, you don't have any control anymore except in prayer."

I knew she was right. I had to let my brothers find their own way. I had enough to figure out for myself.

Jim and the boys made it home in time for dinner, and we

enjoyed spaghetti and meatballs and homemade apple pie. I was beginning to relax, and it felt wonderful.

The next morning after breakfast, we all walked to church. It was a beautiful day. The warm sun made me feel alive and peaceful. Aunt Jane's church was well attended. Since it was a small town, most everyone who went to church went there. There were lots of families, with kids running in all directions, and Jackie's eyes were wide as she took it all in. She went off with Jane to the children's class in the basement. The rest of us found a seat and began to drink in the amazing music that penetrated every corner of the sanctuary.

I felt so close to God at that moment that tears began to run down my face. I had already known He was with me, but since having that outburst with Jack, I had felt a new closeness and peace that I couldn't explain. I knew that everything would be all right no matter what happened with Jack. I drank in everything the pastor said like I had been in a desert without water. From the first word to the last "amen," I basked in the presence of the Almighty.

We collected the girls after church and walked home to a Sunday dinner of fried chicken.

"If I keep eating like this, I won't be able to get in my clothes!" I laughed.

"Just relax, honey. You can starve yourself when you get home."

After dinner, the boys took the girls down to the creek behind their house. It wasn't deep, so the girls could walk barefoot and look for tadpoles. Eli gave each girl a bucket and a net, and off they went. Jackie was having the time of her life. She was so adaptable to her new surroundings that it made me laugh. I had worried for nothing about her ability to deal with new experiences. I had been so concerned that starting kindergarten in the fall would be a tremendous adjustment for her, but now I could put my fears to rest; she would fit right in with no fear at all.

Aunt Martha and I took a seat on the back-porch swing.

"I am so enjoying being here," I told her, stretching my arms.

"We're enjoying having you here, dear."

"You can't even imagine what my life has been like since Mama died."

"I know some of what you've been through, but you've done a tremendous job with Jackie. You should be proud that you've raised such a happy little girl, and you did it by yourself."

"I guess the real struggle is trying to get beyond my feelings for Jack. I took your advice, and I told him how I felt. I also told him he would never be happy with the woman he intends to marry. I said we belong together, and then I turned and walked away."

"You didn't even give him a chance to answer?"

"No, I couldn't look at him after I said all that."

"So you have no idea what he thinks or feels?"

"No, I guess not. I ran to my office and closed the door. I told God I did my part, and now it's His turn."

Aunt Martha began to laugh. I guessed it *was* kind of funny, so I joined in with her.

"Gracie, you are a remarkable young woman. Any man would be blessed to have you for a wife. If this Jack doesn't see what a catch you are, then he doesn't deserve you!"

I had never thought of myself as a catch, but I liked it when she said it. Maybe someone would want me someday. Aunt Martha made me feel good about myself. I hadn't felt that way for years. She was a positive person and very good for me and my daughter.

We spent the rest of the week just having fun. One night, Uncle Jim built a campfire down by the creek, and we roasted hot dogs and marshmallows. Jackie was so thrilled that she could cook her own hot dog that she wanted to cook one after another, but then she didn't want to eat any of them. By the time we got ready for bed, she had to have a bath to get rid of all the goo all over her face, arms, legs, and clothes. It was a great time and a memory for us both that we wouldn't soon forget.

The week flew by, and it was time to board the bus for home. I felt myself tearing up because I didn't want to leave. I felt such peace there, and now I had to go back to the strain of my life.

"Goodbye, Aunt Martha. I swear I'll never forget this week. I love you so much!"

"Goodbye, dear. You're welcome here anytime." She wrapped her arms around me.

I grabbed Jane and held her tight. I was so glad they had made the decision to raise her. She was getting the kind of home and upbringing every kid needed. I looked at Jane, feeling a tinge of sadness. "I love you, baby Jane!"

"I'm not a baby. I'll be in first grade this year."

"Excuse me. I forgot how old you are!"

We laughed and kissed everyone goodbye, and before we knew it, Jackie and I were on our way home.

27

Chapter

Saturday was always our busiest day of the week. It was the day when most families had off work and could come to town to shop. I liked being busy because it made the day fly by, and I didn't have much time to think. I saw Billy as soon as I entered the store.

"Were you able to get along without me?" I said laughingly.

He responded that they had done just fine without me. The coldness was still there, like the frost on a winter day.

"Anything I need to know?"

"There are some invoices on your desk that need tended to, but it was a slow week all in all. I'll be out all next week. It will be good to see if you can run the store by yourself."

I thought that was a strange thing to say, considering I was just his assistant. He handled all the important issues. I helped run the store, but he made most of the decisions.

"Do you *trust* me to run things when you're not here?"

"You have to learn sometime. I won't be here forever."

"Where are you going?"

"I don't have time to discuss this with you right now. I have things to do."

He walked away abruptly and left me standing there bewildered. I guessed I wasn't privy to his thoughts anymore. This was rapidly becoming an uncomfortable situation. I loved my job, but maybe I needed to start looking elsewhere. The day passed quickly, and I was thankful for that.

I headed for home after work, walking rapidly as always. I turned into Alley H, which everyone used as a shortcut. Much to my surprise, there stood Jack, as if he had been waiting for me.

"Where have you been for the past week? I've looked for you every day, and you were nowhere to be found. How could you say what you said and walk away from me? You left me hanging there, speechless. How, after all these years, could you still feel that way about me? Are you deliberately trying to mess up my life, my happiness? I have been upset for a week, thinking about you and all the feelings we had for each other. I didn't need all that drudged up again. I'd put that all aside, and I just wanted to forget about you!" He finally paused.

"Can I speak please?" I asked, raising my eyebrows.

"Yes, of course. Sorry."

"I took Jackie to visit my aunt in Woodburn. I was not avoiding you; I've been away. I told you the truth. I've never loved anyone but you. I truly want you to be happy, but I don't think you'll be happy with Linda. She's the woman your mother picked out for you, but you never wanted that kind of life. I can't believe you're that much different from the boy you were. I believe in my heart that we are meant to be together. I think that was set in stone years ago. Even if we took different paths, I believe our destiny is unchangeable."

"What if I don't agree with you?" he said defiantly.

"Well, then you will marry Linda and live out the life you choose."

"I don't know what to say to you, Gracie. You broke my heart once, and I'm healed now. I care for Linda, and she's good for me."

"Then I guess you should marry her and forget we had this conversation. I've grown up, Jack. I'm not the fun-loving teenager you once knew. I'm careful and sure before I make any decision. When I told you my feelings, I knew it was the right thing to do."

He just looked at me as if all the fight was out of him. I felt sorry that I had weighted him with this news. I loved him so much that I was ready to give him up if that's what he wanted.

"I've got to go, Gracie. I can't talk about this anymore." He turned and walked away, and my eyes filled with tears.

I whispered out loud, "I love you, Jack." I had surrendered this to God, and I was not taking it back. If I had to spend the rest of my life alone, then so be it. I had my family, my daughter, and my heavenly Father to care for me, and that was really all I needed.

Billy took the next week off, and I was on my own running the store. It was not a major reach. The departments were well organized, and each department worked effectively with the others. That's how Billy had it set up, and the system worked.

I was doing very well managing my feelings. I had given Jack to God and had committed in my heart not to take that back. Since Billy was away, all the tension was gone, and I could relax and just do my job. I knew in my heart that I needed to look for another job when Billy returned. But I loved working with people and coming up with new ideas for promotions to increase sales. Ideas would pop into my head in the wee hours of the morning when I was barely awake. It seemed as if God had given me a talent that I wanted to continue to use.

We had put an advertisement in the *Times Leader* about our back-to-school sale. It was coming up in just a couple of weeks, so I wanted to check the ad to make sure the paper had everything correct. I flipped through the pages to reach the ads, and my eyes fell on the society page. The headline caught my eye: "Wilson Family Looking Forward to Son's Wedding." The article went on to tell the details: "Jack Wilson is the owner and operator of the Wilson and Son Furniture Store in downtown Evansville, Indiana. Jack will wed his fiancée, Linda Coleman, on September 15, at 2:30 p.m. at the First Presbyterian Church. It should be the social event of the year."

I was stunned to see it in writing. This made it seem so official. The impact of seeing his name linked to someone else was the hardest part. It was as if someone had cut into my heart and left a bleeding sore. As I thought about it, I knew this was Jack's mother's doing. She was all about flaunting her social status and money to the world. I didn't know much about Linda, but I was sure she came from a family that had social connections and the means to be accepted by Jack's mother. Mildred had gotten what she wanted, what she'd always wanted—her son married to someone who fit her status in the community, and that wasn't me. I let this filter through my mind and whispered to God, *It's yours, Lord, and I won't take it back*.

The week passed quickly, and Billy returned bright and early on Saturday morning. He was much more relaxed and more talkative.

"How was your visit with your mum?"

"It wasn't unpleasant, but she is starting to go downhill. I want to be closer to her to help my aunt since it's just the two of them. It's a big responsibility for two elderly women to live completely alone. I've been considering this all week, and I want to meet with you after work today to discuss some things if possible."

"Yes, of course."

"I need to figure some things out, and it concerns you."

The store was extremely busy with parents beginning to shop for back-to-school supplies. I was helping in the school-supply department until a small crisis developed at the lunch counter. One side of the ice cream freezer stopped working, and everything had to be moved to the other freezer. It took me two hours to get it all moved and organized. Billy called the repairman, but he couldn't get to us until Monday. While I was moving ice cream and trying to fit everything in, I looked up for a second, and there was Jack, eating his lunch and staring directly at me. I thought for a fleeting moment to stop and congratulate him on his approaching marriage, but instead I waved my ice cream–coated hand at him and kept on working. He left soon after that, and I was glad I hadn't said anything to him.

After the store closed for the day, Billy and I met in his office. We were both exhausted and fell into our respective chairs.

"I know you're tired, but we should discuss this now." Billy was very direct, and I could tell this wasn't going to be a personal conversation. "Gracie, I told you about my mother and my aunt's situation. My mother's health is declining, and I'm the only one who can take care of her business affairs. I've decided to accept an offer from another store in my hometown. They need a manager because the store isn't doing too well. They need someone to organize it and turn things around. As you well know, that's my specialty."

"Billy, do you mean you're leaving permanently?"

"Yes. There is nothing holding me here. This store is operating like a well-oiled machine. Anyone could walk in here and take over."

"That's just it, Billy—who will be the manager?"

"That's where you come in, Gracie. I recommended to the head office that they offer you the job." He must have seen the startled expression on my face because he said, "My goodness, Gracie, you've been practically running this store for the past year."

"I know, but it's almost unheard of for a woman to be the manager of a store as big as this one."

"I've already spoken to the guys at the top. They want to come in next week and interview you. Don't sell yourself short, Gracie. I wouldn't have recommended you if I didn't think you could do the job." After a moment's pause, he continued. "And while we're at it, I want to apologize to you for being so cold and indifferent to you. I was hurt, and I withdrew. I guess you only have room in your heart for one man, and it seems like he claimed that territory years ago. I hope everything works out for you and him."

"Oh, Billy, I don't know. Maybe it's just a fantasy. There was an article in the *Times* this week announcing his wedding date for September 15. I do love him, Billy, but if he chooses her over me, then God has something better for me, and I'm at peace."

"Your faith is commendable. I hope you'll be all right because you mean a lot to me, and I want to see you happy."

"Billy, it's so good to have my friend back. I missed you."

"I've missed you too, and I'll help you all I can to get this job. You deserve to have something go right for you and Jackie. The head office guys will be here on Thursday of next week. I want to help you prepare for the interview if that's all right with you."

"That would be wonderful. Thank you."

"You have been a great assistant manager, and I'm going to miss you."

I could see his eyes getting misty, so I hugged him and turned to leave.

"If Jack chooses you, he will be happy the rest of his life."

I gave him a smile and left. At home, I confided in Dad about my opportunity.

He beamed from ear to ear. "Gracie, you could manage the whole country if they gave ye a chance. I'm so proud of ye, lass."

"Billy is going to teach me to say the right things in the interview. Could you stay with Jackie a couple of evenings next week?"

"Ye never need to ask me to keep that sweet lass. It's my pleasure. I will be sorry to see Billy leave. I've grown fond of that lad. I hoped at one time you'd take him for your husband."

"Dad, I love Billy, but not the way a woman should love her husband and not the way you loved Mama. I want what you and Mama had, and I'm willing to wait for it."

"Gracie, your mama was my dream come true, but the pain of losing her was my worst nightmare."

"I know, Dad. I think about her every day."

"Me too. She's never out of my mind or my heart. Maybe it's better not to love someone like that. Then you don't suffer so much when they're gone."

I didn't say anything because I already loved someone like that, and the losing was still a painful possibility.

Billy and I spent two evenings going over all the questions he thought the interviewers might ask. I knew how to run the store. I already did all the ordering and managed the invoices and hired new people. There wasn't anything about the store that I didn't know. I had fired a couple of teenagers once who were playing too much on the job, so I wasn't afraid to confront people who weren't responsible. I got along well with the department heads and every clerk. When a crisis came up, I could think clearly and make decisions.

I'd had to grow up quick when Mama died. I'd learned to think on my feet, and I guessed this ability was a result of all that had happened to me over the years. I had been knocked down many times in my life, but I'd always managed to get back up, which had caused my confidence to grow. Billy said I would do well unless I was passed over solely because I was a woman. Billy said I was as capable as any man, maybe even more.

During the war, women had replaced men in the factories, but federal policies had mandated that men get back the jobs that women once held when the war ended. The country's population had grown rapidly because of all the babies who were born after the war. This was referred to as the baby boom. Women were forced back into the homes to tend to the children, and men took over the workforce. I was a rare breed because I worked and had a child and no husband. My life had never been like other people's. I had always been different and had learned to be independent. I didn't need anyone to take care of me; I could take care of Jackie and myself just fine.

Thursday at 4:00 p.m., two men from the main office walked in and introduced themselves. I was calm and confident because I had surrendered this to God just like I had surrendered the situation with Jack. I felt the blood pumping through my veins as I sat down. I no longer was that intimated girl who felt inadequate and helpless. I had grown strong over the years, and I was ready.

"Miss McDonald, I'm Don Noland, and this is my associate, John Frazier. We are pleased to finally meet you. We have heard many good things about you from Billy."

I said hello, and they sat down.

"We trust Billy because he's one of the top managers in the company. He' been at many stores that were struggling, and he's turned them around."

"I am well aware of how great Billy is. He's taught me everything I know about managing a store."

"Miss McDonald, we are aware of all the accomplishments you've made here at the store. This store has the best sales record in the whole district. We know that you have been a big part of that success. I'd like to ask you a few personal questions if you don't mind."

I nodded.

"I understand you have a child?"

"Yes, Jackie is five years old and starting school in the fall."

"Miss McDonald, what if you decided to have another child? Who would run the store? When you accept the responsibility of being the manager, you must be able to be here day in and day out. Having a child or two could interfere with that commitment." The superior tone of his voice was beginning to make my anger spike.

"Sir, I'm not married. Jackie's dad was killed in the war. But I have family and neighbors who provide a wonderful support system for me."

"It's quite unusual for our company to hire women managers," he said with a cynical tone to his voice.

After that comment, my anger reached its peak and boiled over. "I've helped run my parents' home since I was fourteen years old. I took over the house management and raised my two little brothers when my mother died. I was only nineteen when I had a baby, and I've raised her on my own without a father. While I was pregnant, I worked in a factory to help the war effort. I worked at the soda fountain first and then moved to the housewares department. I very rarely missed a day's work. I was promoted to manager of housewares and ran that department efficiently. I'm a strong woman, and you'll never be sorry if you hire me for this position."

Billy and both of the other men looked at me with their mouths gaping. No one said anything for a full minute.

"Very well, Miss McDonald. We will go back to the head office and let you know as soon as possible."

"It's been very nice meeting you, gentlemen."

That was it. The interview ended, and they left.

"How did I do, Billy?"

"I don't know about them, but you sure amazed me. I'd hire you right now if I were making the decision."

"The world is changing, Billy. I guess we'll see how much."

"Yeah, and you are definitely a world changer."

28
Chapter

Jackie was getting more excited every day, anticipating the start of kindergarten. She already knew everything about it thanks to her aunt Jane. I could hardly believe she was old enough to go to school, but she was more than ready. Jack's wedding was just two weeks away, and I hadn't seen him at all. I assumed he was preparing for the big event. I was still hoping he would change his mind and not make the biggest mistake of his life. I lay awake many nights, praying that God would speak to his heart and show him the truth and that truth would set him free.

Sunday dinner was on the table, and Sammy walked in just as the meal was served, with a giggly young girl following behind him. Mama had always said not to worry about Georgie; he could find a meal whenever he needed to. Apparently, Sammy was no different. He was still playing pool, even though the state had offered to train him to be a watch repairman. Because of his heart murmur, he qualified for free training and job placement. He would be able to get a good job working at a jewelry store and make a reasonable wage. Dad had told him to take advantage of the offer because he would never be able to do anything involving physical labor. Sammy had ignored Dad, as always, and continued to play pool for money.

"Hi, Gracie. What's for dinner?"

"Fried chicken, just like every Sunday, brother."

"I want you to meet my girlfriend, Nellie."

"How do you do? We didn't know Sammy had a girlfriend."

She giggled some more and held on to Sammy's arm. She was a very pretty girl with blonde hair and sparkling blue eyes. Sammy had always been a charmer with the ladies, but he usually liked to spread the love around. This was the first time he had ever brought anyone home to meet the family. Jackie was setting the table and asked if Nellie would like to stay for dinner. It seemed she was the only one using any manners today.

"Yes, I would love to stay for dinner, and thank you for asking."

"How did you and Sammy meet, Nellie?"

"We met at the swing club a couple of months ago. Sammy is a great dancer."

"Sammy is good at a lot of things, and he *does* like to have fun." I rolled my eyes as I turned away.

Dad had been taking an afternoon nap, and he walked into the kitchen in time to hear my last remark. "Yes, our Sammy loves to have fun," Dad said, "and now he needs to learn to enjoy work."

Sammy looked a little embarrassed, but he just laughed it off, as he did everything in his life.

"Did I hear Sammy say your name was Nellie?" Dad was looking at her with a curious eye. He seemed a little skeptical about the kind of women Sammy was meeting at the pool hall and dance halls. "Where do you live, miss? Do you have a job?" Dad was asking questions rapidly and not giving her a chance to answer.

Finally, she caught up with him and began answering between giggles. She was just the same as Sammy. They both laughed and giggled as if everything Dad said was a joke. As it turned out, Nellie was a nurse. She had been through school and worked at one of the local factories as an industrial nurse.

She had a room in a boarding house with three other nurses. Her family lived twenty-five miles out of town, so she had to live in town to be close to her work.

Sammy's expression grew serious, and he put his arm around Nellie. "Dad, I've asked her to marry me. I want you and Gracie to give us your blessing."

Nellie's eyes filled with tears.

Dad nodded, and his aggressive attitude melted into understanding. "Nellie, do you want to marry this boy?"

"Yes, sir. I love Sammy with all my heart," she said with a teary smile.

"Do you know he doesn't have a steady job and refuses to take the training the government is offering?"

"Dad, I decided to take that offer. I'm going to the post office to sign the papers tomorrow. I want to earn a good living for Nellie."

Dad's eyes widened. "So you're serious about taking a steady job?"

Sammy had a rare sober look on his face. He pulled Nellie to him and said, "I love this girl, and I'll do whatever it takes to make her happy."

"All right, then! Let's have our dinner and welcome this pretty lass into the family!" I believe my dad was thankful that Sammy might have found a woman who could get him to take life seriously. The good Lord knew none of us had ever been able to convince him of anything remotely connected to responsibility or work. Dad seemed at peace as we ate dinner. This was his youngest son leaving the nest and learning to fly on his own. I was sure he was thinking of Mama and hoping she was proud of him for taking care of their children.

Dad looked at Sammy while cutting his chicken. "Sammy, I'm proud of you, son, and I know your mama would be too."

"Thanks, Dad. I appreciate that."

Our family was growing again. The news of Sammy's engagement only increased the realization that my baby brothers would both be married before me. How had this happened? Time was slipping away, and I had no idea what was going on with Jack. I fell asleep that night thinking about all of the times we had spent together. I dreamed he was waiting at the altar for me to walk down the aisle.

Sleep came and went, and I woke more tired than when I'd gone to bed. I felt as if a heavy weight was hanging around my neck. I dragged myself out of bed to face a new workweek.

Billy met me at the front door. "I got a call from the head office, and I need to speak with you." His face was flushed with excitement, and we hurried off to our office.

"Gracie, they're going to hire you. There will be a probationary period to see if you can manage everything yourself. They want me to stay for a month to get you accustomed to all the reports and forms that you'll need to do. There are a few things that I do that you're not familiar with. They were really impressed with you! They told me the vote was unanimously in favor of hiring you."

I was stunned to say the least. I felt a lump in my throat, and my mouth was dry. "Billy, you helped me do this. How can I ever thank you?"

"I didn't do anything but tell them the truth. You did this yourself, Gracie. You are an amazing woman, and they are lucky to get you."

Billy left to open the store, and I fell into a chair and cried, all the while thanking God for His unmerited favor. I had a feeling in my heart that this was just the beginning of more blessings that were on the horizon.

I couldn't wait to get home and share the good news with Dad and Jackie. Things were turning around in my life, and I was more than thankful.

"Dad, can you believe they're actually going to allow a woman to manage the store?"

"Gracie girl, I'm busting at the seams with pride for ye. I always knew you were destined for great things."

29

Chapter

The new position of manager came with new responsibilities and accountabilities. Everything that happened in the store fell back on me. I was now the boss and had to know my people personally and be able to trust them. Billy closed the store early one night and had a meeting with all employees to tell them about the coming changes.

"Please have a seat, everyone. I have an announcement to make," Billy said. "I'm happy to inform you that Gracie McDonald will be taking over as your new store manager. I am being moved to a new store in Virginia. You all know Gracie well, and I don't believe anything will change much. Department heads will now report to her, and anything that comes up, she will take care of just like always. She will be hiring a couple of new people to fill her position and a couple of new clerks. Are there any questions? Gracie, do you want to say anything?"

I addressed my associates. "Folks, I know all of you so well, and I appreciate all the cooperation that you have always given to me. This is a new trail this company is blazing. They have never had a woman manager before. I, for one, am happy that women are taking their place in the workforce. It's a whole new era, and I need you all to help me. Anything you need, please come to me. My door is always open."

Everyone clapped, which I felt was their way of giving me a

vote of confidence. I was very excited and nervous. I had a lot to learn in a month before Billy left me on my own.

"Billy, do you really think I can do the job?"

"I have no doubt in my mind. You'll make that store better than it's been, you mark my word."

After I got home everyone was full of questions. "Mommy, are you really the boss?" asked Jackie.

"Yes, sweetheart, I'm the boss."

"Mommy, you've always been the boss of me!" she laughed.

"Well, am I a good boss or a bad boss?" I asked with a smile.

"You're a great boss, Mommy, because you always let me know you love me even when you say no. I think you have to let those people know you love them no matter if you tell them no."

"I will definitely keep that in mind, sweet girl."

That night I fell asleep quickly and didn't even think about Jack. I woke in the morning ready to take on the day. I had such an excitement in my bones. I just knew it was going to be a new day, and something spectacular was going to happen. Billy still had a month to train me in the art of running a successful store. He had a real talent for interacting with people and getting them to do what he needed. I got along well with most of our employees; however, there were a few clerks who appeared uncertain of my ability to manage.

"Billy, I wonder if Joyce thinks I'm not qualified to operate this store the way you did. She's been kind of cool with me since you made the announcement."

"Gracie, morale is one of those areas you need to keep on top of. People do develop attitudes, but if you respect them, they'll respect you. Talk to your department heads. They are your first line of defense, and you need them. This is not a one-man or one-woman job. Everyone has to work together."

I tried to keep a positive attitude and let the store run as it always had. I didn't want to charge in and make changes right away. I had some ideas, but I wanted to wait till Billy was gone and transition them in slowly. I walked through the store constantly, looking at how things were running and talking to everyone to see if they were content with their departments. I told everyone that if they had any suggestions to let me know—I was very open to all and any ideas. I wanted them to know that I was someone they could talk to, no matter what the issue.

Jack's wedding was a week away, and I had been too busy to even think about it. I had peace in my heart about him, and I was glad I was busy. Tuesday afternoon, I decided to try to get home early because Jackie was expected at school for kindergarten registration. Billy said he'd close for me so I could get home in time. I cut down the alley to save time as always. I made the turn quickly, and there stood Jack, leaning against a mailbox, waiting for me. I was stunned and taken off guard, as I always was whenever he appeared unexpectedly.

"Jack, what are you doing here?"

"I'm waiting for you."

"Why are you waiting for me? I'd think you would be getting ready for you grand wedding. According to the paper, it's this Saturday, and it's the social event of the year."

"Yes, it's planned for this Saturday."

"Let me be the first to offer my congratulations."

"Thanks, but I don't want your congratulations. I want you to listen to me. I have things to say to you that I've bottled up for years, and you need to hear me out."

"All right, Jack, but I'm due at the school to register Jackie for kindergarten. Can we do this later?"

"I want you to meet me tonight at seven down on the creek bank, under that tree where you told me you didn't want to marry me. Do you remember?"

"Of course!" I was startled to say the least and leery of where this was going.

Jack was so intense that he frightened me. He wasn't the carefree guy who had laughed at almost everything and had never taken life too seriously. I didn't know what had changed him, but my heart ached to see the pain in his eyes. His shoulders were slumped, and he reminded me of someone who was worn down from carrying a heavy load.

After Jackie's registration, we went home, and I made a quick dinner. Jackie was consumed with excitement about school, so she ate quickly so she could get to her chalkboard to practice her letters.

"Dad, would you keep your eye on her for a while? I need to run a couple of errands."

"Sure, honey, whatever you need."

I got ready and started out, hoping Jack wouldn't change his mind. We had so much history together, and I wanted it cleared up just as badly as he did. He didn't need to start a new marriage with baggage weighing him down. I loved Jack and probably always would, but I had resolved to honor his marriage and end this once and for all.

I arrived first and leaned against a tree, praying. I was nervous but thankful that this was finally going to bring out all of the things that had needed to be said for years. I looked up and saw him walking through the trees. He was moving slowly, with his head down. This was not going to be a joyful meeting for either of us.

"Jack, I'm glad you're here. I hoped you wouldn't change your mind."

"No, I'm seeing this through. You have to understand what it's been like for me."

"Jack, I don't want anything from you. When I told you how I felt that day at the store, it just shot out of me. Even though those were my true feelings, I didn't have the right to assault you like that."

"Gracie, that was a gut punch. You have no idea what that did to me. I haven't been able to sleep or eat right since that day. All I can think about is you and the life I wanted. How can I marry Linda when all I can think about is you?"

I held my breath. "Well … I'm sorry not for what I said but for the way I said it. I had to tell you the truth, no matter how it turned out for us."

"Gracie, I fell in love with you when we were kids. After we parted and I went to the war, so many things happened to me so quickly that I was in shock for a while. I never heard from you, and I managed to seal off my emotions and just deal with the day-by-day sufferings of war, and there were many. I was injured and traumatized for a period of time, but I healed and started working as a medic. That helped me get my mind off myself and focus on the immediate problems and forget the past. I got letters from Mom and my sisters, which I appreciated, but I never heard anything about you. One day I got a letter from my mother telling me you had a child, and she was concerned that it was mine. Of course, I told her that was ridiculous because we had never been together like that."

"Jack, I have never been with anyone except Bo just that one time, and I was drunk and barely remember it. From that big mistake I had Jackie, but she is not a mistake. She is a precious little girl, and I would give my life for her. Please do not dishonor her because of Bo. I never cared about Bo; I just wanted to have fun like most teenage girls. I can't change things that happened, but I am sorry for what you went through, and I am sorry I didn't write to you. I was ashamed, and I hid myself away from everyone. It took God Almighty to change my heart so I could go on living. There was a time when I wanted to die because of guilt and losing you and my mum. Trust me, you're not the only one who has suffered through these last six years."

"Yes, I see that now. You've done pretty well for yourself, considering all the obstacles you had to overcome. You've worked yourself up to an assistant manager position. That's really an accomplishment."

"Actually, I just got promoted to store manager. Billy is leaving in a couple of weeks. I'm the first female manager they have ever hired."

"Wow, now that's an accomplishment. Speaking of Billy, I thought you and he were dating?"

"We did, for a bit, and he wanted to get married and make a life for Jackie and me, but I didn't love him that way. I've never loved anyone that way except ... you."

Jack looked down and cringed, almost as if in pain. "Gracie, I'm in a real predicament. My wedding is this Saturday. Everything is arranged. It's going to be a social extravaganza. Canceling it would affect my business, my family, and of course, Linda. She doesn't deserve to be let down. She is a good woman, and she's been there for me ever since I got home."

"I understand, Jack." I just stood there looking at him, feeling helpless and loving him with every fiber of my being.

He walked toward me. He had never come within two feet of me in all the times we had talked. He took my hand and drew me to him. He put his arms around me and hugged me tight. I was so shaken that I began to weep, softly at first. Then sobs poured from my innermost being, and I clung to him the way a drowning man would cling to a life raft. He held me tight, and I could feel his shoulders quivering, and I realized he was sobbing too. We held each other until the sobbing stopped. When he pulled back, his face was red and stained with tears. I had never seen him cry before, and my heart ached. He leaned down and gently pressed his lips to mine. It was such a gentle kiss. Was it a kiss of farewell? I felt as if he was telling me goodbye.

"Gracie, I will always love you, no matter what happens in our lives. You were my first love, and it was real and eternal."

"Jack, my heart will always be yours. There will never be another who could fill that space."

We hugged again, and he walked me up the creek bank to the road. There was nothing else to say. I understood his business and family obligations. I knew he had a commitment that he had to fulfill, and I loved him more for being an honorable man.

"Goodbye, Jack. Thank you for having this talk with me. I think we'll both be better now."

"Good luck with your new job."

It felt like the final act of a drama, when you're left with all the raw emotions, but the curtain has fallen. We went our separate ways, and I cried all the way home. *God, how am I going to live without him?*

I woke up Saturday feeling a heaviness in my chest. This was Jack's wedding day. This was the day when all my hope for us was gone. He would belong to someone else after today, and I had no right to continue to love him. I walked to work, praying constantly under my breath. The heaviness in my chest increased until I could scarcely get a deep breath. *Lord, how am I going to live with this ache in my heart?*

I opened up the store, and Billy arrived shortly after me.

"Hey, do you think we'll be busy today?" I asked. I was grasping for anything to get my mind off of the wedding.

"Oh yeah, these next two weeks should be as busy as the Christmas season. Everybody's got to get their pencils and new shoes and lunch boxes. We'll be busy all right. What's wrong with you? You look like you have the flu."

"I'm okay. I just didn't sleep well."

The day moved quickly, as Billy had predicted, and I locked up and headed for home. I made dinner and sat with Jackie while she formed letters on her tablet. It seemed all she wanted to do lately was make letters and draw pictures of herself in school with other kids. She was so excited about starting school, and I was thankful she had something to occupy her thoughts. She could read me like a book, so I didn't want her asking me a thousand questions about why I wasn't happy.

Dad was reading the paper, always concerned about the state of our country. I picked up the society page to see what grand events were in the news. I scanned the page and stopped short when I saw a small announcement: "The wedding between Jack Wilson and Linda Coleman has been postponed indefinitely. The family apologizes to the guests for any inconvenience. No other information is available."

I couldn't believe what I was reading. *Jack canceled his wedding!* Surely, this must be a misprint. When we'd parted at the creek bank, I had thought that was the end of us. What had Jack done? My mind raced in all directions, trying to understand. I could only imagine the upheaval in Jack's family right now. *I ask you, Lord, to be with Jack and help them all through.*

30

Chapter

I **went to** work Monday morning confused to say the least. I had no idea what was happening with Jack. I suspected he was probably dealing with the fallout of the canceled plans. I had to interview a young man to be my assistant manager, so I needed to focus. He came very highly recommended by the head office, and I wanted to give him the best chance possible. They had given me a probation contract, so it was very important that I do everything by the book and heed their recommendations. The young man was a local fella. He had managed a small grocery store for the past two years but was ready for something that was more of a challenge. He was just twenty-one years old, unmarried, and smart, or so I had been told. Billy had offered to sit in on the interview since I had never done one before. He had told me that having the right people in the right positions was one of the most important aspects of the job. My employees could make the store prosper or destroy it.

"Welcome, Mr. Bennett. It's nice to meet you. I'm Gracie McDonald, and this is Billy Frye."

"How do you do?" Mr. Bennett seemed pleasant and relaxed.

"I understand you have management experience?"

"Yes, I've worked in retail for the past few years."

"You must have been just a teenager when you started working."

"I actually have been working since I was twelve years old. I did all kinds of jobs to help my mother because my dad was killed in the war. I have two little brothers, and Mom depends on me, so I need a better job."

We discussed everything the job would require and his responsibilities. I tried to pick his brain to see what kind of work ethic he had and if there were any character flaws. I liked him right away and felt he would be a good addition to our store. I liked that he was a man and had worked hard all his life.

"Mr. Bennett, I've enjoyed speaking with you. I will review your references and get back to you in a couple of days. Thank you for coming." I stood up to shake his hand.

Johnny Bennett seemed like a perfect candidate. He was clean-cut, confident, and personable. After he was gone, I asked, "What do you think, Billy? He seems like a hardworking young man to me."

"Gracie, do you think everything he said is true? He made himself out to be ready for sainthood. I get the feeling he isn't being totally honest. We need to call the store where he works and talk to the owner to see what is really going on with this boy."

"Okay, I'll do that."

I spent the rest of the day rolling ideas around in my head about Mr. Bennett and Jack. I needed to learn to read people better. I was somewhat gullible and naive at times. Billy was right; my staff needed to be trustworthy and loyal if the store was going to run efficiently. After we closed, I put in a call to the grocery store where Mr. Bennett worked and spoke with the owner. He was an Italian immigrant and a bit difficult to understand. I asked him if Johnny Bennett was considered trustworthy.

The store owner laughed out loud and abruptly said, "I fired that dimwit six months ago. He was lazy and took food every chance he got. No, he was not a good worker."

Uh-oh. "Thank you very much. I am so sorry to have bothered you." I was amazed at how I had misread this boy.

The workweek continued, and I didn't hear anything from or about Jack. I knew he must be up to his ears in confusion and with angry people trying to understand why all of their plans had fallen apart. I didn't understand it either.

Billy was getting ready to move to his new store, and I didn't want him to go. "How am I going to get along without you?"

"You'll be fine. You need to just jump in and get wet."

"Hey, I meant to ask—how did you know that Bennett kid was lying to me?"

"That's simple. He was just too good to be true. I also watched his body language. He was twitching every now and then, which made me think he was nervous. When someone is trying to pull a fast one, they will be a little jumpy."

"I didn't notice his body language. Lesson learned."

"Have you heard from Jack?"

"No, I think he has his hands full right now. I don't want to be involved in that mess."

"And yet you are probably the cause of that mess."

I didn't have an answer for that, so I hugged Billy and promised to call and write. I would need him as a collaborator when I couldn't figure out what to do. He would always be my go-to guy.

Billy was gone, and I had a new person to interview for assistant manager. This time, a tall young woman walked into my office. She was attractive and well dressed and had a sweet smile on her face.

"Good morning. I'm Gracie McDonald, store manager."

"Good morning. I'm Lizzy Reynolds."

"Please take a seat and let's get started."

I remembered Billy telling me to watch the interviewee's body language and not be deceived by facts that were too good to be true. He had said, *Remember, they are going to tell you what they think you want to hear, so don't swallow everything they say hook, line, and sinker.*

"Are you from the immediate area?"

"Yes, I was born and raised in Evansville. I graduated from high school two years ago. I have been managing a small bookstore that my grandparents own. They were getting tired of coming in every day, so I run it for them now."

We discussed some technical issues concerning inventories and ordering of stock. She seemed smart about business and marketing strategies. I liked her, and even though her personality seemed rather subdued, I felt she would open up and be more herself if she was hired. We spent a few minutes chatting about our lives, just getting to know each other. She was several years younger than me, but I could relate to her desire to start her life and make her own money.

"I feel as if my grandparents are watching every move I make. They want me to manage the store, and yet they don't want me to make any decisions without their approval, and we rarely agree on any of my ideas. Miss McDonald, I really need this job. I promise I'll do everything you ask me to do without question."

"I certainly understand your feelings. Not too long ago, I was there myself. I have to speak to the main office and check your references, but I won't speak to your grandparents. I'm sure that would create an awkward situation for you and your family. I'll call you in a few days with our decision either way. Thank you very much for coming in today."

31

Chapter

I hadn't heard from Jack, and I wondered every day about what was taking place in that family. I imagined that the situation was still pretty raw, and I didn't want to get involved for fear I would be blamed for the breakup. I had no idea what Jack had told his family about me or Jackie. I wasn't even sure if it was a breakup; it might be a postponement, like the paper had said. I was so busy most days with all my new responsibilities that I put Jack in the back of my mind.

Jackie had started kindergarten, and she was consumed with telling me about her teacher and every detail of her day. "Mommy, Miss Jill has us go to reading circle every day, and she reads us the best stories. Today we read *The Doll's House*. I love school, Mommy. I want to be a teacher when I grow up."

When Jackie wasn't in school or telling me about school, she was playing school. She turned one section of the front room into her own little classroom. There was a desk and a chalkboard where she printed all the letters and numbers. Her dolls were her students, and she would play for hours by herself, teaching them to sit still and listen. The dolls didn't have any difficulty with that, but sometimes she wanted me to be her student, and Dad would get caught occasionally. We both tried to avoid the front room when she was playing school. Jackie was the joy of my life. Sometimes I would look at her and wonder how I had ever lived without her. How could something that had been a huge mistake have turned into a wonderful blessing? It was one of God's miracles that I had come to accept and expect.

Lizzy started work the following week, and I spent much of the first few days training her and acclimating her to the routine. I introduced her to the department heads, and she seemed to fit perfectly into our store's personality. She was enthusiastic, helpful, and ready to do whatever I asked of her. I was so thankful that I had made a wise decision. It seemed to wipe out my blunder with Mr. Bennett. I was still having trouble trusting my own judgment when it came to employee choices, but my confidence grew when I watched Lizzy perform her duties with ease and efficiency.

Our office area was upstairs above the main floor. There were three small offices. One was mine, across the hall was Lizzy's, and next to her was the accounting office. Ruth Birch had run the accounting office faithfully for twenty years. She paid our bills and did our bank deposits every morning. She also paid our employees and withheld their taxes. She was a quiet woman but extremely qualified. Billy had said many times that without her we would crash and burn. I got along well with Ruth. She had always been kind to me, and if there were any discrepancies, she told me immediately, and we worked to fix them. I trusted her more than anyone in the store.

Lizzy was down on the main floor with Frankie Marple, our new security man. He was retired from the police force and had lots of experience. He acted as a floor walker, keeping his eyes and ears open for shoplifters. When her other duties were completed, Lizzy walked the departments, doing the same thing. Shoplifters were beginning to target our store, and theft would probably increase during the Christmas shopping season.

I was busy doing purchase orders for the Christmas merchandise. I was absorbed with trying to figure out what would draw people into the store and what promotions would be the most effective when I sensed someone at my door. I looked up, and there was Jack, leaning against the doorjamb, staring at me. My heart did a flip and landed in my stomach. I just looked at him, unable to speak. I hadn't seen him since that night on the creek bank when he'd held me in his arms and we'd both cried and said goodbye.

"Hi. Is the manager available?" He had a twinkle in his eye as he anticipated my reaction.

"Jack, what a surprise!"

"How are you, Gracie?"

"I'm okay, Jack. H-how are you?" I stammered, reflecting the fluttering of my heart.

"I'm managing to put one foot in front of the other. At least that's what they tell you to do."

"I read in the paper that you postponed your wedding. I'm sorry, Jack."

"Don't apologize. I couldn't marry Linda. I didn't love her the way she deserved. She's a good woman, and she needs to have someone who can make her happy, and that's not me."

"I hope I didn't have anything to do with your decision."

"Are you kidding me, Gracie? You had everything to do with my decision. How could I marry someone else when you have been wrapped around my heart my whole life? You're the first thing I think about when I get up and the last thing I think about before I go to sleep. I've done everything humanly possible to put you out of my mind, but nothing works."

Jack closed the door and came behind my desk. I stood and looked into those beautiful blue eyes that were so honest and full of love. Here stood the man I loved and would always love.

"Jack, I know I've caused you pain, and it seems I'm still creating problems for you. I never meant to upset your life again."

He looked into my eyes and shook his head. "Hush. You're not upsetting my life. You've given me my life back. I've lived as only half a man for years, going through the motions of what was expected of me. No one ever cared about my happiness or my feelings. If I had married Linda, I would have spent the rest of my life living up to the life they planned for me. You know me, Gracie—I was never like my family." As he took my hands and continued to look into my eyes, he said, "Gracie, you are my family. My life doesn't make any sense without you."

I felt my heart soar. He was still there—the Jack I knew and loved was still there. He hadn't changed.

I collapsed against him, and we both surrendered to the emotions that had been denied for so long. "I love you, Jack, with my whole heart and soul." We held each other until my mind alerted me to reality. "What are we going to do?"

"Right now, I'm going to kiss you and forget about everything else."

Our lips came together, first soft and tender and then deep, filled with all the passion that had always been ours. I pulled away to get my breath, and he whispered in my ear, "I don't know how I lived these past six years without you. I wished myself dead a few times, but now I'm glad I didn't die. I wouldn't have wanted to miss this moment with you. I want to marry you, and I want to do it soon."

Just as he said that, the door swung open, and Lizzy burst into the room. "Gracie, we caught a shoplifter! Oh! Please excuse me. I didn't know you had someone in here."

Jack and Lizzy looked at each other in complete surprise.

"Lizzy, what are you doing here?"

"I work here, Jack. I'm Gracie's assistant."

We all stood for a moment in awkward silence until Jack spoke. "Gracie, Lizzy is Linda's cousin."

I was speechless. How, with all the people in the whole city, could I manage to hire the cousin of Jack's ex-fiancée to be my personal assistant?

After another few seconds of uncomfortable silence, I took a deep breath and looked at Lizzy. "What happened downstairs?"

"A woman was caught stealing in the cosmetic department."

"Okay. Go back down, and I'll be there as soon as I can."

After Lizzy left, I said, "Jack, I have to go. Please come and see me tonight."

He looked at me with the same old smile on his face. "Wild horses couldn't keep me away."

That evening, I made a quick dinner, anticipating Jack's visit. He had been to my home before but not very often. I didn't know what to expect, and I wanted to prepare Dad and Jackie by explaining a little but not too much. "I'm having a visitor this evening after dinner."

"Who's visiting, Gracie girl?"

"Do you remember Jack Wilson from high school?"

"Yea, isn't that the lad you were so sweet on in school?"

"Yes, I saw him today downtown, and he wants to come by and catch up."

"Mommy, was he your boyfriend?" Jackie giggled and rolled her eyes.

"When we were kids, he was my boyfriend, but a lot has happened since then."

"Do you still like him?"

"I've always been fond of him; he's a really nice man."

"Was he in the war, lass?"

"Yes, he was wounded, and he still has a slight limp. Would it be all right if we sat on the back porch and talked? Maybe you both could stay in the front room while he's here. He may talk about the war, and I don't want Jackie to hear all that horrible stuff."

"Maybe Jackie and I will take a walk to get an ice cream cone. What do you think, lassie? Would you like that?"

"Great, Pappy! I want vanilla with pink and white swirls."

I heard a knock at the front door, and Jackie raced to open it before I could catch her.

There he was, smiling down at Jackie. "Hello there. Is your mommy home?"

"Please come in. Are you Mommy's boyfriend from high school?"

Jack laughed and said, "I'm Jack. Who are you?"

"I remember you from the park. Remember, we have the same name, and I wanted to come to your wedding."

Jack came in and shook hands with Dad. "Nice to see you, Mr. McDonald."

"Nice to see you too. Gracie told us you were in that awful war. Where were you stationed?"

"I was in France most of the time. That's where I got shot. After I healed, I stayed behind our lines and worked in the hospital for the rest of the war. My leg kept me out of any more action."

"All I can say is thank the good Lord you could stay out of that mess, and we're glad you made it home safe."

"Thank you, sir. So am I."

"Jack, would you like a lemonade," offered Dad.

"Yes, sir," Jack said politely. We took our lemonade and I quickly maneuvered Jack to the back porch for fear of what Jackie might ask next or what Jack might say about us. Dad yelled a few minutes later that they were leaving. Jack immediately pulled me into his arms. He kissed me passionately, without restraint.

"Gracie, I missed you so much. I can't think of anything else but you."

"I feel the same."

We held each other, enjoying the moment and feeling the bond forming between us again. I was home in his arms, and this was where I was supposed to be. This was the man I was born to love. I can't even explain the sense of wholeness that washed over me. I had let go and surrendered the situation to God, and He had honored me for my obedience.

"Gracie, I want to marry you, and I want it to be now. We've wasted too much time already."

I looked into his eyes and could see the longing and the love that he had buried for so many years.

"Yes, I'll marry you," I said breathlessly.

He kissed me again, long and slow. When we pulled apart, tears were running down both of our faces.

"Gracie, I see you as my gift from God, and I intend to spend the rest of my life celebrating each day with you."

32

Chapter

I had no idea how things would change with Lizzy. I was her boss, but Linda was part of her family. There had been social gatherings between the families so I knew they were all socially connected. This was an upper class of people that had multiple connections in the community. I assumed Jack's parents didn't know about us, but I had no idea what Lizzy had shared with her cousin and Jack's family. I didn't know what to expect when I went back to work.

The day started out normal, and Lizzy was her sweet, efficient self. As the day went on, I felt the best way to handle the issue with Lizzy was to ignore it. After all, she was my employee; I didn't need to explain my personal life to her or anyone. This was my business.

The weeks moved by rather quickly. Jack and I secretly planned our wedding. It would be small, with just immediately family if they chose to come. We knew that his family had to be told, but the timing never seemed right. One afternoon just before closing, Jack came up to my office looking a little shaken up.

"What's wrong?" I asked him.

"Mother came into the furniture store today right after lunch. Apparently, she had run into Lizzy, and they'd had lunch together. Lizzy told her that she works for you. During the conversation Lizzy shared all about our encounter in your office. She told Mother that we were hugging and seemed to be very cozy with each other. My mother was furious and demanded to know what was going on between us. I simply told her everything and concluded with the fact that we are going to be married in a couple of weeks. I told her she was welcome to come and be a part of the celebration. She stormed out of the store, and that's the end of the story." Frustration and apprehension were visible in his face. He knew, as did I, that the war was going to heat up.

I was rather stunned because I had thought we could ease into telling his parents. I hadn't wanted to shock them with our news. There was nothing to do now but wait and see what ramifications would develop. "Jack, they had to find out sooner or later. Let's pray they accept our decision."

Jack recently had told me that he had accepted God into his life while in France. A chaplain had visited the troops in the hospital where Jack was recovering, and he had prayed with Jack for healing. Jack said a certain peace had come over him during that prayer, and he had never forgotten that experience. He said he'd known after that that he would get through the war and come home someday.

"If I can survive the war, I can survive the wrath of my mother," he said, "put it out of your mind."

Jack went back to his store. I felt I needed to talk to Lizzy and clear the air with her. She was a fine employee and, I was sure, a good person, but this talking behind my back had to stop. I wondered who else she had talked to about me and my personal business.

I caught Lizzy as she was leaving the store, seemingly in a rush. "Lizzy, could you wait a moment please? I want to speak to you before you leave."

"I have an appointment, Gracie. I can't be late."

"I understand, but then I need to meet with you at eight thirty in the morning before we officially open. Is that possible?"

"Yes, yes, of course. I'll be there," she called before turning quickly to go.

I wanted to keep my temper under control and remember that Lizzy was young and just learning to deal with adults and adult situations. I needed to be tactful and considerate and act as a professional.

Jack had been coming by every evening; we couldn't seem to stay apart. My day wasn't complete until he held me in his arms. Jackie was a wee bit confused about it all, so we decided to sit down with her and explain that we were getting married, and she was getting a daddy. I knew it was best to keep the conversation as simple as possible, so I started out by revisiting how her real daddy had been killed in the war.

"Honey, remember how I told you that your daddy was killed in the war?"

"Yes, Mommy. I visit his mommy all the time, and Robert is my cousin and my very best friend. We go to school together every day."

Jack looked at me and smiled. "Not much this young lady doesn't already know."

"She is very aware of everybody's business, I assure you. Jackie, because your daddy is in heaven, I felt you needed a daddy here on earth—someone you can talk to and play with, someone to love us and keep us safe. Jack is going to be my husband and your new daddy."

Jack smiled at her and humbly said, "Jackie, if you'll give me a chance, I want to make you and your mom happy. We could be a family, and I promise I'll take good care of you and your mommy."

Jackie looked very serious and pensive. "Will you live here with us every day?"

"Yes, I'll live with you and your mommy every day, maybe in a different house, but all together."

"That's the way Robert's family lives. His mommy and daddy sleep in the same bed. Will you sleep with my mommy?"

I knew it was time for me to step in because Jackie could get very descriptive and detailed in her questions. "Jackie, the main thing is we would be a family."

I looked at Jack, and he had a twinkle in his eye that started my heart racing. The corners of his mouth curved as a smile began to spread across his face.

Jack turned his eyes back to Jackie. "Do you think we could be a family, sweetheart?" Jack had a hopeful look on his face, knowing he had to endure her scrutiny.

"What will I call you?" Jackie asked, thinking.

"You can call me anything you want, but I hope someday you'll call me Daddy." Jack sure knew how to melt my heart.

After twenty more questions, I felt Jackie had a grasp on how our lives were about to change. I loved Jack so much, and he was being so patient with all the changes we were about to make in both of our lives.

After Jackie went to bed, we talked to Dad about everything, including Jack's family's disapproval. My dad had always been the voice of reason in my life, and he continued to encourage us. "If you two love each other, then that's all that matters. Everything and everyone will come together eventually."

I loved my dad so much. Leaving him was going to be very difficult. He was the one who had taught me to wait for the man who would love me the way he loved my mother.

Jack was responsible for finding us a place to live and ordering the furniture we would need immediately. I had contacted Pastor Kirk and arranged for the church. We would get married in the sanctuary and have a brief reception in the basement. I had invited Aunt Martha, Jane, and their family and my brothers and their families. Sammy would bring Nellie because she was soon to be part of the family. Jack had invited his parents and his sisters, but no one had responded yet. He was currently living with his parents, but they were not on speaking terms.

I had bought a dress for Jackie and a dress for myself. She

would be my maid of honor, and Dad would be Jack's best man. We didn't really care about the wedding; we just wanted to be together. After all of the years we'd spent apart, we couldn't wait to become man and wife.

The next morning, I met Lizzy precisely at 8:30 a.m. We took a seat in my office. I asked her to explain her side of this situation.

She timidly began, "Jack was engaged to my cousin Linda for the past year. I attended several gatherings with Linda and Jack's family. Linda and I are very close. I was to be her maid of honor in her wedding."

"I understand you were probably upset when you saw Jack and me together. Did you know that Jack and I were sweethearts back in high school?"

"No, I had no idea that you even knew each other."

"We got separated during the war. There were some things that drove us apart, but we never stopped loving each other. Jack and I belong together. We never meant to hurt anyone. I know Jack thinks very highly of Linda and is thankful for her support after he came home from France."

"Linda is very hurt right now."

"I'm sure she is, and I'm sorry about that. What I'm more concerned with is your revealing of private information about me. Why did you tell Mildred about Jack and me?"

"I never meant to, but she started talking about Linda and Jack and how upset she was, so everything just seemed to tumble out of my mouth. Before I could stop myself, I'd told her about you and Jack in your office. She was furious and stomped out of the restaurant. Gracie, I'm sorry—please don't fire me! I need this job, and I love working here with you!" She was close to tears.

I felt sorry for her. "I have to be able to trust you. You're not just a clerk; you know the inner workings of this business. I need to know that what you hear will stay confidential."

"Gracie, I am so sorry. It will never happen again. I promise."

"Thanks for meeting with me. As long as we're on the same page, I think we can move forward together."

"I understand. It won't happen again," she said gratefully.

This was the first time I'd had to reprimand an employee. I felt as if I had done a fairly good job, considering how angry I'd felt in the beginning. I was adapting to my role as store manager little by little, but I also was aware that I myself was on a probationary period. How was the head office going to respond to my approaching marriage?

33

Chapter

Jack and I were so excited about our plans. After Dad and Jackie went to bed, we talked well into the night about anything and everything. I was very concerned about how Jack and Jackie would respond to each other after the wedding.

"Jack, do you think it will be hard for you to start our marriage with a five-year-old child? Jackie is a demanding little girl, and she has had all the attention her whole life."

He pulled me into his arms and looked into my eyes. "I am going to say this only one time, so you need to listen carefully. I don't care where we live or who lives with us. I don't care what we eat or where we go or what we do. All I care about is having you near me every day and in my arms every night. Nothing else matters to me. Do you understand?" He looked at me playfully.

"You know Jackie is Bo's daughter. Does that bother you?"

"Jackie needs a dad, and I'm willing to step up and fulfill that role. What could be wrong with that? How could that possibly bother me? I love you, and I love Jackie, and together we'll work through any difficulties."

The days passed slowly, and our nights were filled with making plans and longing for the time when we could be together as husband and wife. The store was running smoothly, and the holiday season was approaching, which required promotions and window displays. Lizzy was a great help, and I taught her everything I could to take some of the burden from me.

Jack and I would be married long before Christmas, so I wasn't concerned about the wedding conflicting with the holiday rush. We still hadn't heard anything from his parents. He and his parents avoided each other most of the time. Jack didn't seem to care whether they came or not. He said the only ones he needed at our wedding were me and him and maybe the pastor.

Jack had found us a small house about four blocks from where I lived now. This would allow Jackie to stay in the same school. He set up the kitchen with a new refrigerator and stove and ordered an electric-powered washing machine that had a galvanized tub to make washing clothes so much easier. He even bought an electric dryer with a glass window. I was completely amazed; I didn't even know such appliances existed.

"I want you to have as much help as possible with the household chores because you'll be working at the store all day, and I don't want you working all night around the house," he said.

I loved his attitude. His way of taking care of me made me feel loved and cherished.

We met at his store one afternoon and picked out our bed and a dresser. I wasn't picky about material items since I wasn't used to the best of everything. I managed with whatever I had and was content.

"You are nothing like Linda and my mother," he told me. "They spent hours going over the kind of drapes we would need in the living room and how large the kitchen table should be to fit at least six people."

"I like nice things, but I can make do with what I have as long as everything works properly. I don't like broken appliances or clogged pipes."

Jack laughed at me about the pipes. He had been laughing quite a lot lately. He was my old Jack again, the one who laughed about everything. The lines were gone from his brow, and the worried look had been replaced with a calm sense of peace. He knew exactly what he wanted, and there were no questions or hesitations. He was charging forward and not looking back. I loved his calm assurance because it gave me a sense of peace and security that I hadn't had in years.

A week before my wedding, I arrived at work a little earlier than usual. The store was still closed, so I took a little time to grab a coffee and look over the invoices on my desk. The Christmas merchandise had arrived, and I needed to think about changing displays and having things delivered to the various departments. As I was considering this, the phone startled me. I picked it up on the second ring, and Billy's cheerful voice came across the line.

"Hi, Gracie. Glad I was able to catch you before your day started. How are you doing?"

"Actually, I'm great, Billy. How are you?"

"Things are moving along quite well. I am finally getting this place organized. I want to share something with you that you need to know. I know about your marriage plans."

This caught me off guard. I purposely hadn't shared any of my future plans with anyone on the job except Lizzy, and she was sworn to secrecy. "Yes, Jack and I are getting married next week. How did you find out?"

"The head office called me yesterday and gave me the news. Gracie, they are concerned because one of the stipulations of your employment was your being single. Remember, you told them you were not married and didn't plan on having any more children. They want to be sure you are able to be on the job and will not be bogged down with family."

"I understand, but I'm able to be married and still run this store."

"I'm just giving you a heads-up that you're going to get a call, and you need to be ready to respond."

"How did they find out?"

"I was told some woman named Mildred Wilson called them and gave them all the information. Do you know a Mildred Wilson?"

My face grew hot, and I clenched my teeth. "Yes, I do. I know her very well, unfortunately. Thanks for the call, Billy. Talk to you soon." I was devastated that Jack's mother would try to find a way to have me removed from my job. How could this woman hate me so much just because I loved her son? *Help me, Lord!*

Within the hour, the call came.

"Miss McDonald speaking."

"Hello, Miss McDonald. This is Don Noland from the head office. How are you today?"

"I'm fine. Just getting ready for the Christmas season."

"Yes, we are all getting ready for the rush. I need to speak with you on a more personal level. It has come to my attention that you may be planning to be married. Is that true?"

"Yes, I am," I answered in my most professional tone.

"Do you remember the agreement that we discussed, about you being a single woman? We were very concerned about your ability to run a store and a family at the same time. Do you remember the conversation?"

"I certainly do remember, but what makes you think I can't be married and still run this store?"

"Well, we don't want to burden you with too much," he replied in a mildly condescending tone.

I rolled my eyes and hoped he could feel it through the phone. "I assure you, Mr. Nolan, I will not be burdened with running this store and being married at the same time. I signed a contract with you when I took this job, and nowhere in that document did it state that I couldn't get married. I don't see how my personal life has anything to do with my employment status. Have you been looking at my reports concerning the store? Do you have any complaints about the numbers or my job performance?"

"No, you've done a fine job. We have no complaints."

"If my marriage interferes with my job, I will be the first one to make a change. I'll quit in that case—you won't have to fire me."

"Calm down, Miss McDonald. No one is thinking about firing you. We'll be in touch and ... congratulations on your marriage." There was that tone again!

I was angry and frustrated but not with Mr. Nolan. I was angry with Jack's mother for sneaking behind my back and trying to destroy my life and my career. How could this woman live with herself or even sleep at night?

34
Chapter

Our wedding day arrived. It turned out to be a clear, crisp October day with few clouds and a bright sun. I quietly thanked God because I felt it was a day signifying the bright future that lay ahead of us. Our wedding wasn't until late afternoon, so I had the whole day to prepare Jackie and myself. I had taken off work for the whole weekend, and I kept Jackie home from school on Friday. Jack and I would have two days for our honeymoon. We weren't planning to go anywhere except our new home. Jackie would stay with Dad for the weekend, and we'd go back to work on Monday morning as usual.

I didn't tell Jack about his mother's attempt to get me fired. Why add more anger to the already brewing resentment he felt toward his parents? I didn't want to think about anything remotely negative on the happiest day of my life. Jack and I had resolved that whatever his family did concerning us would not impact our lives. We would live our lives with them or without them.

"Mommy, what does it mean to become a husband and a wife? I heard Jack say the other day that he couldn't wait for you to be his wife. What's a wife?" Jackie was a very inquisitive little girl. I couldn't believe how emotionally mature she had become.

"Honey, remember in Sunday School when Miss Sophie talked about how God saw that it wasn't good for Adam to be alone, so He gave him Eve? God realized that Adam needed a woman for a wife so he wouldn't be lonely."

"Is that why you're marrying Jack? Because you're lonely?"

"I'm not completely lonely because I have you and Pappy, but I am lonely for a husband. That's how God intended it to be, so He put the need for love between a man and a woman in our hearts. Someday you'll find someone that you love and want to marry, and then you'll understand. Love comes in many forms, but it all comes from God."

"I love you, Mommy, but I don't love my teacher the same way I love you. Is that what you mean?"

"That's exactly what I mean. You are such a smart little girl." I smiled at my sweet daughter.

Dad drove Jackie and me to the church at three. We dressed in the Sunday school room in the basement. I got Jackie into her dress and put flowers and ribbons in her hair. She had dark hair and blue eyes like Bo, so her bright daffodil-yellow dress stood out in amazing fashion. I felt a tinge of sadness thinking that Bo would have loved to have seen his daughter and realized what an amazing child she was.

Mrs. Kirk helped me get into my dress and fixed a short veil to my hair. "You're a beautiful bride, Gracie. Your mum would be so proud of the fine young woman you are."

"Thank you. I have your husband to thank for all he's done for me and my family. I'll never forget the kindness you both have shown me through very difficult times."

"Ahh, forget all that. We just want you to be happy with your new husband."

Dad knocked on the door and said it was time. As my dad walked me down the aisle to meet Jack, I felt such a strong presence of God. It was as if He had wrapped me in His arms and was washing away all the loss and pain. I was filled with a peace like I had never known. Everything I had been through, as tragic as it was, had made me into the woman that God had wanted me to be and had prepared me to be the wife that Jack needed.

Dad put my hand in Jack's. I looked up into his tear-filled eyes, and he whispered that he loved me. I smiled back at him as my own tears began to run down my face. The ceremony was brief but very emotional. We had waited so long for this moment; we couldn't have stopped the tears if we tried. Cake and punch were served afterward in the basement of the church as everyone congratulated us. Jack's family did not attend, but we barely noticed their absence. We were so happy that nothing could have ruined our day.

We made our way to the little house Jack had rented for us. After he opened the door, he suddenly scooped me up in his arms and carried me through the door. "Welcome home, Mrs. Wilson," he said with a smile.

My heart was beating so fast that I thought it might burst out of my chest. As Jack put my feet on the floor, he pulled me to him and looked deep into my eyes. "Gracie, I promise I'll do whatever it takes to make you happy. You and Jackie are my family now, and nothing and no one will ever come between us."

I knew it hurt him that his family had let him down, but I promised in my heart to love and support him all the more to make up for their refusal to accept me as his wife. Our weekend together was more than I ever could have imagined. We never left the house but spent the days and nights in each other's arms. I understood now what my mum and dad had felt for each other and why they were so closely knitted together. When God said that "they shall become one flesh," He knew that marriage would form a bond between a man and a woman that nothing could tear apart. "Whom God hath joined together, let no man put asunder."

35
Chapter

We moved Jackie in on Monday evening and spent most of the night setting up her room and, of course, her little school. She was so happy to have her own room and kept running from room to room to look at all the new furnishings. She was obsessed with the washer and dryer and asked Jack over and over how they worked. He explained it three times before I redirected her to her room to line up the books on her desk. We were beginning a new life, and everything seemed perfect. Jackie helped me make her bed and put her clothes away. Her room had a closet just big enough for her clothes to fit perfectly. Her pink bedspread matched her curtains. The small lamp by her bed gave the room a soft glow.

"Mommy, my room is beautiful. Pink is my favorite color."

"I'm glad you like it, honey. A girl's room is her own very special place. I never had a room of my own when I was growing up, so I'm really glad we could make this for you."

"Thank you, Mommy. I love you, and I love Jack too!"

Jack had been standing in the doorway, watching and listening to our conversation, and I saw the tender look in his eyes as Jackie talked about her room and then made the comment about him. I knew in my heart that God would form a bond between the two people I loved most in the world because He was faithful to those who loved Him.

The morning came as usual, and I had to get up early to get

everyone moving. We would drop Jackie off at school and drive into work together.

When I entered the store, I felt as if I was walking on a cloud. I had taught Lizzy to open the store so I wouldn't have to be exactly on time every day. She had been perfect since our discussion, and my faith in her was beginning to grow.

The holiday season was fast approaching, and we had a considerable amount of stock that needed to be marked and distributed to the various departments. I knew it would be a busy day. I assigned the department heads the task of getting the new holiday stock priced and put on the shelves while the clerks checked out customers. If business was slow, they could all pitch in and rotate stock and get the new merchandise displayed.

It seemed like a good plan until Margie from the women's department came down with a stomach virus and had to go home. Then the sink at the lunch counter sprang a leak. I had to call a plumber, and it took a half a day to fix. It seemed as if everything that could go wrong did. I ran from one department to another, trying to help get all the new merchandise in place.

I was on my way to the stairs to my office when Mildred, Jack's mother, grabbed my arm. "So you think you've won, do ye?"

I turned around, completely taken off guard.

"Do you actually think Jack is going to reject his family because of you? We have ways of dealing with him that you can't even imagine," she sneered.

"I'm sorry you're upset, but Jack and I love each other, and we're making a life together, and you're going to have to accept it."

"I'll never accept you into our family!"

"If you don't accept me, then you won't have Jack either, and that would be a shame for you both."

I could see the rage rising in her face, and suddenly I felt very sorry for her. She was a mother trying to control a son who didn't want her interference in his life. She had planned his whole life for him, and now all her plans were crumbling at her feet. She glared at me for a second and turned and walked away.

I don't know how I got through the rest of the day. I sank into my desk chair and closed my eyes. *Lord, help Jack's mother accept our marriage. She needs us, and we need her.*

At the end of the day, after the store was closed, I heard Jack coming up the steps. "Sweetheart, are you ready to head for home?" he asked as he entered my office. I must have looked like a train wreck because he said, "What happened to you?" He put his arms around me and drew me close.

I just collapsed against him from sheer exhaustion. "I've had a really bad day."

"Yeah, I can tell. Come on, let's go home."

I didn't tell Jack about his mother's visit. He had already been hurt enough by his family, and I didn't want to add fuel to the fire. Whenever their names came up, I saw his jaw tighten. I hated that his family didn't support him, and it felt like my fault.

We began to develop a rhythm to our new little family. Jackie and Jack were learning to enjoy each other's company. He began reading to her at bedtime, and she would reciprocate using her little reader from school. I had to say she was very smart; she could read everything the school sent home without hesitation.

One evening after dinner was over, Jack pulled me aside and asked if we could talk while Jackie was playing in her room.

"My dad stopped into the store today. He wanted me to know that he is thinking about hiring someone to take over management of the store. He said he has been thinking about this for a while, but now he feels it's time to make a change."

"Does that mean that he's firing you?" I said with alarm.

"He didn't come right out and say that, but I think in a roundabout way, that's what he meant."

"Jack, I can't believe they would ruin your life because of me. What did I ever do to make them hate me so much?"

"You didn't do anything, honey. It's all about control. My family has always wanted to control my life, from as early as I can remember."

"What are we going to do?"

"I don't know, Gracie, but I'd rather lose my job than lose you. I don't care what they do. I'll find another job and take care of my family any way I can. I don't want you to worry about this—it's my concern."

"I'm going to pray for them, Jack. They must be miserable." I didn't hate Jack's family. God had put compassion in my heart for them, and I truly wanted them to love and accept us.

We were growing as a family. I loved Jack more than I had ever thought I could love anyone. I found myself becoming more and more dependent on him. My independent ways were melting into a comfortable intimate union that was bonding us more with each passing day. I knew nothing would ever tear us apart.

Jackie was relaxing and finding her place, and she often allowed herself to call Jack "Daddy." I watched the warmth fill his eyes when this happened. His patience and kindness brought such joy to my heart that I had to turn away so Jackie wouldn't see the tears running down my face.

We had no word from Jack's family. He continued to manage the store. He had always thought the store was in his name; however, after speaking to his lawyer, he discovered that was not the case. Max Malone was the attorney for the whole family, including Jack. He told Jack that the business was in his father's name and would come to Jack only when his father passed. The store was owned by Tom Wilson, and Jack was just the manager. Tom hadn't changed the will yet, but anything was possible. Jack continued to say he didn't care about the store. Jackie and I were the only things that mattered to him, he said; he'd take care of us if he had to dig ditches.

36

Chapter

The Christmas shopping season was in full swing, with only three weeks left. Our store was packed most days. I didn't have time to worry about anything except getting through the rest of the year with strong sales and increased profits. I was in contact with the head office on a regular basis, but they never brought up my marriage situation. I had a feeling that they were watching my sales reports and making sure I could carry the load as a married woman. This motivated me to work harder to juggle my work and my family. I was not going to let down this company that had given me a chance to succeed in a time when most women never got the opportunity.

The last week before Christmas Eve, I decided to keep the store open till nine each evening. I'd had a brainstorm one night as I was trying to get to sleep. I figured if we were open later, it would boost sales and profits. Any employees who volunteered would work, but it was not mandatory for anyone. Amazingly, most volunteered without being coaxed. It turned out to be a tremendous success for sales but a very long day for everyone. Jack would pick me up at nine every night after closing, and I would drop into bed completely exhausted.

Jack was rubbing my feet as I lay propped up in bed. "Sweetheart, do you think this is a good idea?" he said. "Your feet are swollen."

"I know it's hard right now, but it's only a few more days. I have to show the head office that I can do this job just as well as any man."

"I'm just worried about you."

"Don't worry. I'm tougher than I look," I said, winking at him.

"I know, but when you hurt, I hurt too. Remember, you're bone of my bone and flesh of my flesh, swollen feet and all."

I smiled. "Jack Wilson, do you have any idea how much I love you?"

"I guess not. Would you like to tell me?" He curled his body into mine, and we drifted off to sleep.

The next day, I was up and at it again. If I hadn't had the adrenaline pumping, I might not have gotten out of bed, but I was on a mission, and nothing was going to stop me until it was accomplished. Somehow by Christmas Eve, we had met and exceeded our sales goals, and we closed at our regular time.

I had things to do at home for our celebration. This was going to be our first Christmas as a family, and I wanted it to be special. We attended the candlelight service at church and got Jackie to bed early so Santa could come. Jack and I wanted to have some quiet time together to exchange gifts. After Jackie fell asleep, we sat on the sofa. He gave me a gold heart on a chain. "Gracie, read the inscription," he said.

I turned it over, and engraved very small on the back were the words "You have my heart now and forever." I cried yet again. It seemed one of us was always crying about something wonderful! Our love for each other was so pure and passionate that we couldn't hold back our emotions.

On Christmas Day, everyone gathered at Dad's house for dinner. Georgie was no longer working at the pool room. He had a permanent job printing the race results at the track in the summer. In the winter he worked at the print shop. Things were better between him and Mary Ann. Sammy brought Nellie; they were still engaged and planning a wedding in the spring. Dad roasted a turkey and made stuffing, and we all brought the trimmings. I so enjoyed the family time and the rest.

Jack was busy as the new year got into full swing. He had to do inventory and taxes. Working with the accountant and his employees took a great deal of extra time. Linda no longer worked at the store, and he had never replaced her, so much of the inventory fell on him. He stayed late several nights to get it completed. He called me one night from the store to say he had received a call from his lawyer, he wanted to meet with Jack the next morning. I knew my husband pretty well, and even though he swore his family's rejection didn't bother him, I knew better. Anyone who was exiled from their family, no matter what the reason, had to feel hurt. I prayed for Jack, believing God would somehow make this all right and heal his family.

The next day, Max, the family attorney, told Jack that his family was considering cutting him out of any inheritance and perhaps even hiring a new store manager. Jack said the attorney was very apologetic and really didn't understand why all this was occurring. Max felt that Jack was doing a great job and that the store was doing well. No rational person could grasp this situation because Jack's family were not rational people.

I held Jack tight as he shared his conversation with Max. I had to fight off the guilt and sadness. I was responsible for all of this. I was the one keeping Jack from his family. I didn't know what to say or do.

"Gracie, I know how you think, so understand right now, this is not your fault. I love you. I have always loved you. You are a part of me, and my life has no meaning without you. Don't start taking on blame and making this your fault. There is only one party to blame, and that's my parents. This is their fault." He knew me so well.

"What are you going to do?"

"I don't know yet, but we'll figure it out."

I knew Jack would have to think this through on his own, so I stayed as quiet as I could. I prayed a lot and again surrendered it to God. I'd get up every morning and whisper, "I surrender this day to you, Lord. Help Jack to figure this out." This was how I lived my life now. I had learned the hard way, but I had learned.

Time passed with no word. Jack and I lived on pins and needles, waiting for a call from Max Malone. We were uncertain about the store and Jack's family. My sales and profit reports were excellent, but my probation period was almost over, and they were going to make a decision about giving me a continuing contract. We prayed every day that God would remove the uncertainty so we could relax and enjoy our new marriage and our new family. Jack and I kept all our fears from Jackie. She was thriving, calling Jack Daddy most of the time now and reading fluently. I realized more and more what a gift from God she was.

37

Chapter

I was working in my office, completing and filing inventory sheets, when the phone rang. It was Jack.

"Gracie, I just got a call from Northwood Hospital. They said my dad had a heart attack, and he's in intensive care. What should I do?"

"You need to go to the hospital now, and hurry. I'll get Lizzy to close the store this afternoon and meet you there as soon as I can." I was stunned. Tom was only fifty-four, and he had always seemed strong and robust.

I arrived at the hospital after Jack, and as I entered the waiting room, Jack was holding his mother in his arms. She was weeping uncontrollably. His two sisters hovered around her, holding on to their boyfriends' hands. They glanced at me, and I could see the fear in their eyes.

I walked over to Jack and put my hand on his shoulder. "What have the doctors said?"

Mildred looked up and tried to get control of herself.

Jack looked at me with desperation in his eyes. "They said he had a massive heart attack, but he's resting comfortably right now; they'll know more in the morning. They want to give it twenty-four hours before they say anything definite."

"Well, we're just going to pray for the next twenty-four hours that God will heal him."

Mildred glanced at me and said, "What do you know about prayer?"

I looked her right in the eye and said, "I know a great deal about prayer." I pulled Jack aside and told him I was going to arrange for Annie to pick Jackie up from school and keep her all night. I intended to spend the night at the hospital, praying for Tom.

Jack, his family, and I sat quietly in the waiting room. They allowed Mildred to go into Tom's room every couple of hours. I prayed silently for several hours, and then I made a bold move: "Could we join hands in a circle and pray out loud?"

Everyone just looked at me for a moment and didn't move.

"I believe we need to do this. Tom's life is on the line here, and we should do everything possible to help."

After a few seconds, everyone reluctantly stood up, and we joined hands. No one said anything, so I took the lead. I was beyond caring what any of them thought of me; I just knew we had to pray for this man and not let him slip away into eternity without God.

"Heavenly Father, we lift up Tom Wilson to you. He's in bad shape right now, and he needs you to touch his body and heal him. We know you love him, and we know you're the healer, so give us a miracle here tonight, and we'll be forever grateful. Amen."

The girls and Mildred were crying softly, and Jack hung his head, praying to himself. I had prayed once before for a miracle, for my mum, and it hadn't turned out the way I wanted, but this was different. My mum had been ready to leave this earth, and Tom Wilson was not.

Along about 6:00 a.m., the charge nurse came out and said Tom's vital signs were good. He was not out of the woods, but things were beginning to turn for the better. The nurse suggested that we all go get some coffee and breakfast. I decided to call Annie to check on Jackie and let her know what was going on at the hospital. I also asked her to call Pastor Kirk to have the church pray for Tom.

We settled ourselves in the hospital coffee shop, feeling completely drained and exhausted. I tried not to say too much because I knew I wasn't totally welcome at this family gathering. Jack held my hand and stayed close to me. He sensed the coldness from his family and wanted me to know he was with me. We had a wee bit of breakfast and wondered when we would know something concrete.

Jack said, "If his vital signs are good, then that means he's getting better, right?"

"I'm not much of a medical person," I said, "but I believe in prayer, and I've got my whole church praying."

Mildred looked at me directly. "When did you become a religious person? I never knew you attended church."

"I always attended church with my mother. She was a strong woman of faith. Since my daughter was born, I've grown so much closer to God. He's my best friend."

She just looked at me and didn't respond. It wasn't necessary for her to say anything; she had a look in her eyes as if she had just seen me for the first time.

Around 10:00 a.m., the doctor came into the waiting room and said Tom was turning a corner. He was awake, and the family could visit him for a few minutes. Jack and I didn't go in because we didn't want to upset him, but we rejoiced because our prayers had been answered, maybe in more ways than one.

Jack and I waited until everyone had come back. Before we left, I grabbed Mildred's hand and looked her in the eye. "It looks as if God answered our prayers," I said.

She squeezed my hand and cried. I felt nothing but compassion for this woman even though she had tried to destroy me and my marriage.

Tom Wilson was a strong man, and day by day, he began to recover from a massive heart attack that should have killed him. He was moved out of the intensive unit to a private room.

Jack and I stayed away because we didn't want to upset him and possibly make matters worse. Mildred was at the hospital every day and kept Jack updated on his father's condition. He wasn't out of the woods completely. The damage to his heart would require him to alter his lifestyle after recovery. That meant he needed to slow down and not work as much. Mildred told Tom that we had been there the day it happened, and we'd prayed for him. We still didn't know where we stood with this family. They remained quiet, and we kept our distance.

Mildred called Jack at work one afternoon and said his dad wanted to see him. Jack didn't know what to expect, but he knew something was stirring. I prayed constantly that this family could find reconciliation. No one should go through life angry with the parents who bore them or with the child they created. They were a family, and nothing and no one would ever change that reality.

"Gracie, I want you to go with me. You're my wife, and we're in this together. They need to see us as united; if they want to see me, then they need to see you too."

"I don't think that's a good idea. Your dad just had a serious heart attack. He obviously wants to talk to you privately, and that's how it should be right now."

I had no idea what his dad wanted, but I didn't want to complicate the matter. I wanted them to speak freely, and I didn't think they could do that with me in the room. God was the only one who could fix this family, and His methods were beyond my understanding.

After work that day, Jack went straight from the furniture store to the hospital. I went home and put dinner in the oven. He hadn't called or come home when dinner was ready, so Jackie and I ate by ourselves.

"Where's Daddy?"

"He went to visit *his* daddy in the hospital."

"Is his daddy sick?"

"Yes, he is really sick with his heart."

"Should we pray for him, Mommy?"

"We've been praying, honey, and he's getting better."

"Can we visit him?"

"No, not now. He needs to rest."

"How come we never see Daddy's family? Are they my grandparents too?"

She was making connections, and I was stumped for answers. "Jackie, we'll talk about this when Jack's dad gets better. Sometimes grown-up situations are … complicated."

She seemed satisfied with that answer for now.

When it got to be nine thirty, I began to feel concerned. I hoped Tom hadn't gotten upset and had another episode. I heard the car pull up out front and breathed a sigh of relief. Jack came through the door looking as if he had been crying.

I hugged him, and he smelled of nervous perspiration. I held him close for a few minutes, and he collapsed against me.

"Was it bad?"

He pulled away, and I saw a slight smile pull at the corners of his mouth. "It was bad at first, and then it was good."

"Is your dad all right?"

"Yes. Physically, he's doing well. He may get to come home next week, and he has to learn to take things easy."

"Okay, get to the point: what did he say about us and the store?"

"Your prayers are working. He wants to see you tomorrow after work. We talked about you and me and the store. He was thankful that we prayed for him. He seems different, Gracie. I think the heart attack shook him up quite a bit. I think he's scared to die and realizes he came very close, and he's rethinking his priorities. When you have a brush with death, everything changes. That's what happened to me in France when the chaplain prayed for me, and I've never been the same. No matter how great you think you are, you have to remember there is someone greater, and He's in control. I told my dad about my brush with death, and he hugged me and cried. It broke my heart to see him like that, but I think something good will come out if it. Don't you always say all things work together for good?"

"Yes," I said, kissing him. "You catch on fast."

We held each other until Jackie ran into the kitchen.

"Daddy, it's time to read!'"

"Okay, pumpkin, I'm coming."

I knew that God was working this out in His time and in His way.

The next day, Tom was sitting up in bed when Jack and I entered the room. His color was good, but he looked thin and drawn. He smiled as we approached his bed. Mildred was sitting in a chair near him, holding his hand.

Tom smiled. "Nice to see you, Gracie."

I smiled and nodded. "I'm glad you're feeling better," I said.

"I guess I have you to thank for that. I understand you led a prayer group on my behalf."

"We all prayed for you, Mr. Wilson, and God honored our prayers."

"Call me Tom … please."

I smiled and glanced over at Mildred. She was quiet and staring at the floor. A thought hit me like a lightning bolt: Tom Wilson had never been my adversary; it had always been Mildred. She was the one who set the attitudes in her home, and the rest followed.

"Tom, I am thankful you're doing better. If there is anything we can do, please let us know, and we'll continue to pray for a speedy recovery."

"Thank you, honey. Just take care of my boy, and I'll be thankful for that."

"Mom, let me know when they release him, and I'll come and drive you home." Jack was trying to be helpful and let them know he was still their son and loved them.

"Thank you, dear," said Mildred. "We are hoping it will be in a few days." Mildred said nothing to me, but she hugged Jack and kissed his cheek. She had her boy back, and she was happy for the time being.

I left the hospital with mixed feelings. I was thankful for Tom's recovery and his kindness to me. There had been a dramatic change in his attitude toward me and toward God. Their family had always been social-status Christians. They had attended church consistently to have friends and to network for potential business opportunities. They had never been genuine in their faith. Maybe Tom had changed, but Mildred had not. Her attitude toward me was the same.

Jack said very little on the way home. He knew I was bothered by his mother's behavior toward me, but what could he do? This was his mother, and I was his wife, and he was caught smack dab in the middle.

Chapter

Jack's dad had been home from the hospital for a month. He had been working a couple of days a week and improving with each passing day. Jack had visited with him at the office and at his parents' home a few times. I was never invited, and I said nothing about his parents except to ask for the occasional update on Tom's health. Jack was slightly defensive concerning them, and I knew he didn't have any idea how to straighten out this quandary in which he found himself. Jack was a loving, good son and a wonderful husband, so no matter what he said or did, he was going to hurt someone.

Max Malone called one afternoon and told Jack that his dad had decided to put all the business concerning his will and the store on hold for now. Tom wanted to rethink things and make sure his decisions would be good for the company. I imagined he was having a conflict with Mildred about what to do about me and our marriage. As far as Mildred was concerned, the only thing that had changed since Tom's heart attack was that she had more of an inroad to her son.

One afternoon a call came in from the head office. "Mrs. Wilson, it's Don Nolan. How are you today?"

"I'm great, and you?"

"Fine, just fine. I'm calling to let you know that we are very impressed with your yearly sales and profit reports. Your store was one of the top ten of all our stores."

"Thank you very much, Mr. Nolan. I'm glad to hear that."

"We are also happy to tell you that a continuing contract is in the mail. Welcome aboard! If you would please sign it, make a copy, and mail it back to us as soon as possible, we would appreciate it. We're honored to welcome you as full-fledged store manager."

"Thank you so much. This means a lot to me. I know you took a chance on me, and I want you to know I'll do my best to live up to your expectations."

"I believe you will."

I called Jack immediately and told him the good news.

"Gracie, that's wonderful! I'm so proud of you! We'll celebrate tonight."

I heard someone talking in the background. "Who's there?"

"Oh, Mom and Betsey were downtown shopping, and they just stopped in for a quick hello."

"Oh great, I'll let you visit. See you tonight."

I couldn't fight off the feeling that Jack's mother was working hard to sabotage our marriage. She was so sweet to Jack but all the while was pulling him back into her grip. She was a scheming woman, and I had no idea what was up her sleeve.

I walked through the next few weeks trying not to think about Mildred and her undermining ways that dug at the foundation of our marriage. The tension was building between Jack and me. He was caught in a vice, and I was one side of that steel trap, and I didn't know what to do. I didn't want to come between Jack and his family. I didn't want to put him in a position where he would have to choose. I tried not to talk about it, but it was like walking through mud in combat boots. The heart attack had changed Jack's dad, but his mother was another story. I couldn't understand why she hated me just because I loved her son.

Valentine's Day had always been a special day for Jackie and me. We always celebrated with cards and candy. Jackie loved to make cards for everyone in the family. We were excited this year to share the day with Daddy Jack. I had Dad bring Jackie to town on Saturday so we could surprise Jack at his office with balloons and treats. I left work early, and Dad met me outside of Jack's store.

Jackie and I couldn't wait to burst into Jack's office with our celebration. As we approached the door, I heard voices. I recognized Mildred's voice as she laughed about how great it was to have all her children together for Valentine's Day.

Jackie pushed open the door and yelled, "Surprise!"

Mildred was standing with her daughters, holding balloons in her hand. Jack looked startled; he had never expected to have all the women in his life in the same place at the same time.

Jackie, being the least daunted female in the room, ran behind Jack's desk and jumped into his arms. "Happy Valentine's Day, Daddy! We wanted to surprise you. Are you surprised?"

"Yes, sweetheart, I couldn't be more surprised." He made eye contact with me, and I smiled, knowing he was speaking the truth.

Jackie kissed Jack on the cheek and threw her arms around his neck. "I love you, Daddy!"

Mildred and Jack's sisters stood motionless, unable to ignore the scene before them. It was an awkward moment but very telling. Mildred was able to see that Jack had a family that loved him, and it was out of her control.

Before anyone could speak, Jackie asked, "Who are all of these ladies?"

Mildred stepped forward. "I'm Jack's mother, and these are his sisters, Betsey and Susan."

Jackie thought for a moment and said, "So ... you're my new grandma?"

Mildred answered coolly, "I'm not your grandma because Jack isn't your real dad."

I gave an audible gasp. What was this cruelty?

"Oh, I know that. My real dad died in the war, but Jack is my adopted dad, and I love him very much. So that *does* make you my adopted grandma. I want to visit you at your house so I can love you too."

If God had come down and spoken to Mildred Himself, it wouldn't have been clearer. The simple truth was that you loved people just because they *were*, not for any other reason. Jackie had learned that in Sunday school. Jackie turned to Jack and continued her chitchat as only little girls could do while her words hung in the air like fog in the morning.

Mildred and her girls left shortly after that, making an excuse about an appointment. I said nothing, and Jack continued to focus on Jackie as a diversion from the uncomfortable atmosphere in the room. The scab had been pulled off the wound, and now we had no choice but to deal with the oozing sore.

Jack and I sat up in bed that night and began the conversation that neither of us wanted to have. "Jack, I don't know how much longer I can deal with your mother's attempts to draw you away from me. She has been trying to control you again by acting like the sweet, loving mother who just wants her boy happy."

"What do you want me to do, Gracie? They're my parents, and my dad almost died. Do you want me to cut them off and create another shock to my dad and his bad heart?"

"No, I don't want you to hurt your family, but do you expect me to live my life on a tightrope, not being accepted as your wife and excluded from your family, while they fall all over themselves to draw you away from me? I'm not stupid, Jack— your mother wants to destroy our marriage and maybe even me. I never told you this, but she is the one who notified my head office about our marriage. That's why they called me with a reprimand after our wedding. She also has come to my store and threatened me." Tears were welling up in my eyes, and I could feel myself beginning to come apart at the seams. "Do you want me to move back in with my dad? I could have our things packed up in one afternoon and be gone."

"Gracie, stop! You know I don't want you to leave! I love the life we've made together. I never want to be separated from you."

"My Bible says when two people get married, they leave their father and mother and are joined to each other and become one flesh. Never does it say a parent hangs on and tries to destroy the marriage. What your mother is doing is wrong, Jack; can't you see it?"

"I know I have to deal with her. Just give me a little more time. I promise I'll fix this."

I felt better after our talk. It was like steam being released from a pressure cooker. Jack didn't say much about it for a few days, and I prayed constantly that God would change Mildred's heart toward me and my daughter.

39
Chapter

A few weeks passed, and little had changed with Jack's family. Tom did tell Jack that he would try to talk to Mildred, but we knew she ruled the family, and Tom was still recovering his strength from his heart attack. I had learned a long time ago about surrender, and now it was time again to give it to God and let it go.

Jack was busy at work ordering the new spring line, and I was managing Woolworth's and caring for a very active daughter who never ceased to amaze me with her emotional intelligence and her instincts about people. I loved it when she would say, "Mommy, its's not hard! You just love God and love people."

Jack had been to see his mother a few times since the Valentine's Day debacle. According to him, she was cold and unrelenting. He told her that we were a family, a unit, and she could either accept us all or lose him. I was proud of him and his willingness to stand up for Jackie and me, but I knew it hurt him deeply. I continued to pray and believe that God had a plan to work this all out.

Spring was rapidly approaching, and we were all busy getting ready for Sammy's wedding and the busy Easter season. The wedding was scheduled for the first of April. Nellie's family probably wouldn't make it. We had learned that her parents didn't speak English and were poor farmers with a large family.

Nellie was the oldest and had landed a scholarship for nursing school.

When the wedding day arrived, our family were the only ones who attended, and Jack and I stood up for the couple. Sammy and Nellie giggled their way through the ceremony, and it turned out to be a joyous occasion. They had a tiny apartment not far from us, and we blessed them with a beautiful bed from Jack's store.

My store did huge business this time of year, with the Easter Bunny and the colored baby chicks drawing people from both sides of the river.

Jackie was very excited because she was soon going to graduate from kindergarten and be promoted to first grade. It was a milestone in her life, and it consumed her day and night. She wanted a special dress and shoes because she had a major role in the ceremony. She wanted to keep her part in the program a secret, but if her excitement was any indication, the event should be a blockbuster. Jackie's school served a large part of the population in our town, so her having a speaking part in the graduation ceremony was quite an honor. It frightened me just a little because she could be very outspoken and sometimes shocking in her insightful views about people and how they should behave. Her teacher told me that they had given her a script but that she also would have a few moments to say whatever was in her heart. That was the part that scared me! Jackie wanted to invite everyone she knew, including Jack's family, Aunt Martha, and of course, her mentor and favorite person in the world, Jane. Jack didn't mention the event to his dad because he didn't want to stir up conflict. It was easier to just play it down and get through it.

The magical day finally arrived. Jackie got up early so she could lay out her new pink dress and black patent leather shoes. She was beyond excited. "Mommy, do you think everyone will be proud of me?"

"Yes, honey, I think everyone will be very proud of you."

"I'm so glad my whole family will be there. I wish Daddy Jack's family would come. I prayed they would."

"Don't be disappointed if they don't. Remember, they don't know us that well." I had been telling her this same thing for weeks because she continually asked why they didn't like her and why they didn't visit us and why we didn't go to their house. I had prayed my explanations would satisfy her, and they did temporarily, but the topic always came up again a few days later.

Her excitement grew as the day progressed, until it was time to make our appearance. I left Jackie with Miss Jill, and we all took our seats in the front row. The program began with the children leading us in the Pledge of Allegiance and one verse of "The Star-Spangled Banner." They sang two of the songs they had learned during the year, and then the recitals began. Several children recited prepared remarks, and then it was Jackie's turn. Miss Jill introduced her, stating that she had the best grades and best attendance of all the children and that was why she had been chosen to give a speech today.

Jackie stepped up to the microphone, and I could feel my heart in my throat. She recited the prepared remarks perfectly and then moved on to her personal thoughts.

"I want to tell everybody what I am thankful for today. First, I am thankful for my mommy and daddy Jack. They love me and give me food and a room of my own. Next, I'm thankful for Grandpa McDonald and Grandma and Grandpa McAllister. I am thankful for all my family that's here tonight. I am also very thankful for my Grandma Wilson who is here tonight to see me graduate. I love her very much, and soon I will be going to her house so she can get to know me and learn to love me too."

Jack turned his head and saw his mother sitting with another woman in the back of the room. Tears filled my eyes and spilled down my cheeks. I could sense my mother speaking through my daughter's lips. Jackie had the same spirit and attitudes as my mum. It didn't matter what anyone said or did; they both always came back sweet and loving.

The program ended, and we all moved to the school library for cookies and punch. Jackie hugged everyone and thanked them for coming. She was the first one to see Mildred coming through the door. She ran to her and threw her arms around Mildred's waist. "Thank you for coming, Grandma!" She grabbed Mildred by the hand and pulled her to where we stood. "I knew my Grandma Wilson would come because I prayed that she would."

Mildred was at a loss for words but managed to respond, "I guess God answers prayers for little girls in unusual ways."

"Grandma, can I come to your house and visit you?"

"Yes, we'll have to arrange that soon." Jack's mother had a different expression on her face than usual, not so hard and angry. She told Jack later that she had come with her friend whose grandchild was graduating and had not realized Jackie would be in the same class.

I wouldn't say Jack's mother changed instantly, but there was a crack in her wall of hostility after that night. Jack's dad decided to leave the store in Jack's hands, as he had originally intended. He kept Jack in his will, and they worked together as they always had. They would maintain a harmonious relationship until Tom's death a few years later. Mildred invited Jackie to her house, and they indeed became great friends. I was invited for holidays and tolerated most of the time.

——— ❈ ———

I think back over my life and remember my youthful selfishness and the plans I had, how I wanted to do everything my way and in my time. I didn't consider that God might have had a different plan all along. My daughter became my greatest blessing, and God replaced my mother with her, as if He knew I needed someone in my life who would show me how pure love worked. The similarities between Jackie and my mother confounded me daily. My daughter's way of thinking and her lack of judgment toward people spoke volumes to me. The mistakes I made and the heartache I brought on myself were erased. I always remember that my weaknesses were what drove me to Him, and His love superseded all my shortcomings.

My dad will always be on a pedestal in my eyes. During the worst times in my life, he never judged or condemned me. He always took care of me and supported me in every way possible. We might never have had a lot of money, but we always had a family who took care of their own. I guess that stemmed from our strong Scottish heritage. We were tough and could fight passionately, but we could also love with the same passion. In six years' time, I grew into a woman who sacrificed the need to fulfill her plans to hear what God had to offer. Wisely, I chose to do things God's way and surrender those things I couldn't understand. Mama always said God would always work everything out, in His time and His way. She was so right about so many things.

As I said, Mildred Wilson tolerated me until Michael Jack Wilson was born. When we brought this eight-pound little bundle home, everything changed drastically. She wanted to visit often and participate in welcoming the beautiful boy God had given us. Her attitude toward me changed as well. She seemed to have a newfound respect for me and went out of her way to compliment me on my skill as a mother. I forgave her and worked at forgetting all of the injustices she had brought about in my life.

After Mickey was born, Jack stood at my bedside, and we both stared at him in total amazement. Jack cried when he first took him in his arms. "I never thought I'd ever have a son, Gracie. Thank you for giving me such a wonderful gift."

"Thank you for being such a wonderful husband."

We laughed and cried in those first few moments, so caught up in the miracle of a new life that we had created together.

Jack was a very proud daddy. I often caught him looking at

little Mickey as if he couldn't believe he was real. He told me one night that he could scarcely believe God could create something so small and yet every part perfect. Jackie was amazed with her new baby brother. She longed for him to be old enough so she could teach him his letters and numbers because, as she often said, she was going to be a teacher someday.

After Mickey was born, I didn't work anymore; I was content being a wife and mother and taking care of my family just as my mother had. My life had come full circle, and I felt complete, ironically, in doing all those things I had run away from as a girl. I just wanted to stay home and cook, care for my children, and wash Jack's socks.

When I was a child I spoke as a child, I thought as a child, I reasoned as a child. When I became a [woman], I put away childish things.
—1 Corinthians 12:11

Printed in the United States
by Baker & Taylor Publisher Services